CONQUEST

HARALD HARDRADA

Barry Upton

1

HARALD HARDRADA - THE LAST VIKING

HARALD HARDRADA - THE LAST VIKING

Reader Review of Harald Hardrada

With a surface-level knowledge of the Battle of Hastings, and having seen the Bayeux Tapestry, I delved into Barry's book with a lot of curiosity about the untold, and partly imagined, past of Harald Hardrada (a man I only knew of from his famous 'final image'). This book is an immensely enjoyable speculation into his formative years, and it is always refreshing to read a protagonist that isn't instantly likeable! despite his flaws, you are drawn into Harald's tale and must see it through to its inevitable conclusion. **An exciting read for those who are intrigued by our ancient past. ******

(Deborah E Wilson, author of "the Artist's Muse")

HARALD HARDRADA - THE LAST VIKING

Conquest is the first series of historical fiction written by Barry Upton.

Details of the earlier novels, plays and musicals can be found on the website: https://barryuptonauthor.com

or by scanning QR code below

What readers have said about earlier books:

A really enjoyable read…

The characters are clearly and realistically defined…

Astute understanding of the trauma of adolescence.

Thoroughly enjoyed reading this book…

Sometimes disturbing and sometimes sad but a gripping, well written book right from the start…

Hard to put down!

Please add your review on the Amazon site.

HARALD HARDRADA - THE LAST VIKING

CONQUEST...

... is a trilogy of Historical Novels, centred around the momentous and tumultuous year of 1066; three titles each focusing on a key figure in the story of the Conquest of England.

The first starts in Norway where **Harald Sigurdsson**, already King of Norway sets his eyes on conquest. Harold Hardrada who became known as "the last Viking".

The second looks at the rise of Harold Godwinson, later Harold II, "the last Saxon", and his rise to power before his defeat at Hastings.

The third focuses on William "the Bastard", the Duke of Normandy who feels he has legitimate right to become King of England.

Conquest tells the story of the most significant year in English, perhaps even European history, through the eyes of its three principal protagonists.

HARALD HARDRADA - THE LAST VIKING

Conquest – Harald Hardrada

Norway was never enough! Harald Sigurdsson grew up knowing that his destiny was to be King of Norway. But his ambition went far beyond. After Cnut's death, he fought to win back the lands the tyrant had captured - Norway, Denmark and England. The story leads him from his childhood in rural Norway to his death on the bloody fields at Stamford Bridge.

He honed his ambition and his skills fighting in Constantinople and adopted the epithet "Hardrada" - hard ruler - or stern counsellor, which he preferred. Harald was a brave and courageous Viking warrior, but he was ruthlessly ambitious. Nothing - and nobody - would stand in his way. In a period of exile, he fought as a mercenary for Grand Prince Jaroslav of Kiev-Rus. He married Elisiv, the Prince's daughter and she fuelled his ambitions.

HARALD HARDRADA - THE LAST VIKING

Conquest: 1 Harald Hardrada is a novel, first in the series focusing on the momentous year 1066. It draws on the great Viking Saga which records his life, offering insights into the man and his times.

ᚺᚠᚱᚠᛚᛉ ᚺᚠᚱᛉᚱᚠᛉᚠ

It is not my role, as a novelist of historical fiction to change facts, only to invent fictions. Much of what is recorded here can be verified by reading *King Harald's Saga.* Little is known of his early life, which gave me scope to explore how Harald Sigurdsson's character was moulded and shaped to become the ruthless, ambitious man known as "the hard ruler". I have tried, where I can, to use place names that would have been familiar to eleventh century people, rather than their modern-day equivalents. While the story is rooted in the sagas, it is my invention, and I make no apology for this being a work of fiction.

I hope there is enough fact to be of interest to scholars of the eleventh century, and enough fiction to delight those who enjoy a good story.

1066

HARALD HARDRADA - THE LAST VIKING

WE HAVE ALREADY LEFT OUR MARK; SCARBOROUGH HAS FALLEN. The treacherous mouth of the Humber welcomes us. Three hundred ships set sail from Orkney, and all but two have arrived. Their sailors survived the storm, rescued by their comrades, but their ships adorn the seabed. The sandbanks, hidden from our view, wait to wreck us and ditch us into the cold Autumn river, deceptively gilded by the early morning sun. We flow up this river of molten gold, sails lowered, oars beating a rhythmic pulse. On either bank, north and south, stand our cousins who welcome us. We had first seen them at Danes Dyke, the green scar cut into the cliffs, as we had journeyed southward along the coast. Our first thought was that this was an assault, but we saw their arms waved in salute, and knew that these were our cousins. These ships of ours are not a conquering army; we are liberators, come to free our people from the yoke of Angle tyranny. We bring them their true King. We can hear them rather than see them. Mist rising from the wide river obscures their faces. We know they are there from their rousing cheers.

On the King's ship, ahead of us, with its Raven sail, the captain reads the charts, made for us by these cousins who fish the waters and know its dangers. Without them we would surely all have perished on the sandbanks that guard the entrance as well as any harbour chains. We have lost one more ship on one such spit, but its crew and soldiers have swum ashore and joined the thronging crowds. I can see the King, his head adorned with horned helmet, glinting gold from the rising sun. He stands tall and still at the prow of his ship, so that serpent and man become as one body.

The river narrows where the charts show the Humber ends and the Ouse begins, and we can see both banks more clearly. The shouts are louder: their faces holes of sound; their arms waving welcome.

HARALD HARDRADA - THE LAST VIKING

And we can see, too, the army forming; farmers with scythes and axes, running along the bank to keep up with us. We had been told that we would be met with warm welcome and willing men. And so it is.

Our cousins have lost their Norwegian features. Most have dark hair and sallow faces, brought about, no doubt, from the close bonding with the Angle people, native to this country, when they arrived many years before. But there is no doubting their Viking hearts.

As the sun arcs its way to lead rather than follow us, we draw alongside the northern bank. There are still many miles to go, heading northwards along the Ouse towards the great city of Jorvik. The King had forbidden them to give it the name York. This was an Anglo-Saxon name, given at the time the city was lost with the death of the great Eirik Bloodaxe. We all know the stories. They had fuelled the journey across from Norway and set us on fire and ready to fight. Jorvik will be restored to its Viking past. Then we shall march south, and all of England will fall.

The ships are tied up alongside wooden jetties, built in preparation for our landing. Food and fires greet us, as well as songs and celebrations. But I stay aboard and watch as the Viking army is welcomed as long-lost brothers: hugs with distant cousins who will soon be brothers-in-arms. King Harald himself is encircled. His name is shouted. His Raven banner is hoisted high above the moot hall, crudely erected but bearing some resemblance to those from home. He stands and speaks, this mighty king who has come to bring Danelaw to all of England. He is cheered as he calls them brothers. They have waited for this day. We are in England.

Alongside the bank two small boys play with wooden swords, as their nurse calls them to eat. They parry and prod backwards and forwards, with roars, too high pitched to be fierce, except to each

HARALD HARDRADA - THE LAST VIKING

other. They remind me of earlier, more innocent times. The nurse takes one by the hand and leads him inside.

1016 - 1030

I watched you, boy, at play.
I saw it in your eyes.
How you were made for greatness,
How you were made to rise.
You grew, and I could see
The man you would become.
The mighty warrior, king of all,
Whose name would span all time.

BOYS

HARALD HARDRADA - THE LAST VIKING

Brenn Gaarder held his hand tightly. Of course, the boy had seen the mighty King Olaf before. He was, after all, his step-brother though she was sure he was confused by this. How could his brother be this mighty king? Her mistress, Queen Ásta, went before her into the huge chamber, shepherding the boys' older siblings. His two sisters, Gunnhild and Ingrid were at the front, clinging tightly to their mother's skirts, while Guthorm and Halfdán, his older brothers held wooden swords in their hands and tried to look brave. But she had heard them crying and fearful, as they were driven along the huge corridor that led to the Great Hall. The youngest boy brought up the rear clutching the hand of Brenn. Not that he was overawed by it all. It took a great deal to upset him, and even more to make him fearful.

This was a special day. It had been a special time. King Olaf was returning home, after three years of his reign, after conquering the rebels. And his mother was eager to welcome him. The servants had laboured for weeks in preparation, and they had been sent out far and wide to gather in the best of everything. There were holes in the fields where the roots had been pulled up in their hundreds; huge carcasses had been loaded onto the carts which giant oxen pulled along the tracks leading up to the farmhouse. The boy had watched them arrive; he had asked her:
- *What does it mean, Brenn? What is it all for?*
- *King Olaf is coming. Haven't you heard?*
- *Mother said we were to be on our best behaviour. She said my brother was coming to see us.*
- *Yes, your brother is coming. And there is to be a huge feast. The whole town is invited. Animals have been killed, and roots have been dug up.*

HARALD HARDRADA - THE LAST VIKING

Brenn could see his confusion. His brothers were Guthorm and Halfdán. Why would anyone make such a fuss over them?

- *King Olaf is your mother's oldest son. He is king of the whole of Norway.*

She watched him as he took it all in. Of course, the boy knew of King Olaf; he knew that he was his mother's son, but it was hard to think of him as his brother.

- *Will I get to meet him?*

- *Tonight. At the feast in the Great Hall. All of you will meet him. Are you afraid?*

- *Why should I be afraid? Is he a bad man?*

- *No, but he is a mighty king, and he has killed so many of his enemies...*

- *Am I his enemy?*

Brenn looked at him. She smiled and smoothed the lines on his forehead. Sometimes the boy looked older than his years. For a three-year-old he was wise and brave, not at all like his siblings, who, though older than him, were content to play on the farm and often ran back to the hall in tears after a fall, or with blood from a cut finger, where they sought out their mother for comfort. But this boy was different. He spent most of his time with her, Brenn, roaming through the woods. She remembered him one time, watching as a boar crashed through the thickets, without a whimper, without a murmur. He just stood, wide-eyed as the boar rushed past him. Brenn had been sure the boy's gaze had diverted the beast. Her heart had pounded, more afraid of the reprisals the boy's death would bring than from the tusked snarling creature. But he had stood his ground and the boar had avoided him. No, the boy was brave, there was no doubting it. He was also wayward, unwilling to do exactly as he was told.

Queen Ásta had taken her to one side.

HARALD HARDRADA - THE LAST VIKING

- Stay with him, Brenn. He will be good with you. He is such a difficult boy, and the king will not tolerate his waywardness. Stay with him. Make sure he behaves. It is an important day for us. My son, has not met his siblings for some time and I want them to create a good impression.

Brenn knew what that meant. King Olaf had no heir, and there were rebels on all sides who would sell out Norway to the Danish invaders. If he were to be killed, who would succeed him? Guthorm was the next eldest but still too young and his mother would have to protect him until he was old enough to succeed. He was a royal prince, and she needed the king to accept Guthorm's claim.

- Keep him busy during the day and bring him to the Great Hall in the evening. Make sure he understands. That boy is so wilful!

Brenn had to admit he *was* wilful, but he was intelligent and curious too. In her opinion, the boy would make a much better, a much braver and a much wiser king than his older brothers. But her opinion counted for little. Brenn knew her place. She was a servant, a wet-nurse; no more than that. And she would do her best with the boy, or it would go badly for her.

Armed guards stood outside the giant doors. There were lighted torches in the recesses either side of the door and shadows danced along the walls, making Brenn shiver. But the boy's hand was steady. The two girls were close to tears, and she could tell that Guthorm and Halfdán were doing their best to be brave. Even the queen looked nervous and her hands shook. But the boy was calm. Perhaps, mused Brenn, he was too young to be afraid. The guards looked at the queen and threw back the doors. Light, heat and noise flooded the corridor and all eyes turned to them. It was Gunnhild who broke ranks first and ran straight to the king. Suddenly, the room was silent, and Brenn felt that the air had been sucked from the room. The king stood. He was tall and erect, powerful like the mighty oak, and yet all sinew and grace like the ash. The guards around him drew their swords.

- *Come, gentlemen, sheathe your weapons. There is nothing to fear here in Ringerike. We are home, and here we are loved by all. And none more so than my little sister, Gunnhild.*

He caught the girl midway through her leap towards him and swung her high above his head.

- *So little sister. Is this the way you greet your king?*

And he placed her down on the table and she knelt coyly before him. All the while, Brenn watched her mistress, heard her sharp intake of breath, and then saw her smile. The girl clapped her hands wildly and suddenly the whole room took it up. The applause was rapturous, and Gunnhild kissed King Olaf's outstretched hand. The queen knelt before her son, who moved clear of the table, swinging Gunnhild between the guards, before placing her on the floor beside her mother.

- *Welcome, my son. Welcome, my lord. Welcome, my king.*

Olaf helped her onto her feet and looked at his step-brothers, studying each in turn, as they were kneeling.

- *So. These are my heirs?*

The room fell silent. They had all heard the stories. Many had joined in the ribaldry, making fun of the king's impotence, though never in his hearing. They lived longer that way. The king had married but there was no heir. *It is a punishment from God,* he had maintained, *for marrying the illegitimate daughter of Olav.* Ásta knew otherwise. Queen Astrid, her daughter-in-law, was barren, and would never give him an heir.

HARALD HARDRADA - THE LAST VIKING

- Come, mother. Let us sit together while the children enjoy the feasting.

And the noise grew again in the Great Hall. And together they sat, son and mother, King and Queen, their heads close together, and they laughed together, and the children ate greedily pulling at the cooked flesh with their teeth, ignoring the vegetable roots. Brenn sat on the other side of the boy. He ate too, but his eyes were fixed on the king. He chewed slowly. And Brenn watched him.

The daylight was fading when at last the children were sent to their beds. Brenn and the other women led them from the table. They were nearly at the giant doors when the king called to them.

- I want the boys to stay. Just for a moment. The girls may go to bed.

Queen Ásta looked up from her place beside him.

- Surely the youngest can be left to go with the girls. He is so young.

Brenn felt the boy twitch.

- I want to stay, mama. Let me stay.

Brenn tried to lead him out. The king looked into his eyes and smiled. He saw the spirit in the boy.

- Let him stay. He and I are strangers. I want to get to know him as I know his brothers. Let him stay.

Brenn bowed and waited at the door.

- Boys. Come here.

They gathered round him.

- I have a game for you. More than a game. It is a trial. Our mother is right. She nags at me, warns me that I must have an heir. Otherwise, she says, all the deaths, all the bloodshed will have been for nothing. And she is very wise, your mother, very wise. And God expects it too. So here you are, and I shall see which of you is best equipped to follow me. I have three tests for you.

HARALD HARDRADA - THE LAST VIKING

We shall start tomorrow at dawn. Meet me at first light on the edge of the woods, beyond the village.

Olaf waved his hand, and the brothers left the room. Guthorm and Halfdán looked for their nurse and she took their hands and led them through the dark corridors. In the torchlight she couldn't see the tears in their eyes. The boy didn't wait for Brenn. He made his way to the chamber which he shared with his brothers. Brenn caught up with him as he reached the door. They went in together. His brothers were climbing into their bed and their nurse was smoothing the blanket. Brenn took the boy's hand.

- What did he say? What did the king want?

- We are to have a trial tomorrow. The king wants to test us, a sort of game. At daybreak tomorrow.

- All of you boys?

- All. Goodnight, Brenn.

She looked at him, smiled and swept her hand through his straw-coloured hair. She knelt in front of him, their faces level. His eyes were bright and blue. His jaw was set firm.

- Goodnight, Harald. You will be a fine king.

The mist still hung above the valley bottom and dripped from the trees. Brenn watched the three boys as they made their way down towards the grey woods. She pulled her cloak around her in attempt to get warm. She still felt the hands of her own boy – Dag, born at dawn and named for it – whose hands had been clinging to her all night. She had unwrapped herself from his grasp, climbed from her bed and watched from the covered doorway as they descended into the wood. They stopped at a signal from one of the king's own bodyguards; they waited there, on the fringes of the wood, then one behind the other they disappeared.

Later she recalled what she had seen and heard of the trial, telling Ásta so that she might understand what had happened.

- *Guthorm led them into the wood. The King had hidden himself behind a giant oak. In front he'd laid out a net trap and both Guthorm and Halfdán walked straight into it. The King pulled them upward, the two boys hanging loosely in the net. Then the King lowered them down and as they clambered out the King simply stood and stared at them, a fierce warlike stare. Both the boys ran away shaking and in floods of tears.*

Ásta had seen the state they'd been in, even the next morning.

- *The king can be terrifying when he chooses to be. What about the boy?*

- *Harald had escaped the net, by running off just at the last moment before it was swung. He climbed a tree and waited for his brother to come and seek him out. He jumped down just as he passed, and landed on the King's back. The King shook him off, laughing at the boy's impudence. He gave him the stare, but the boy stood his ground. The soldiers with the king were amazed by his bravery. They say he never flinched, but stood staring back at the king. King Olaf went up to the boy and pulled his hair, but young Harald never moved, never cried out. Instead, he grabbed his step-brother's moustache and tugged at it. The guards all moved forward. But the king roared with delight, lifted the boy into the air and shouted to all of them:*

- *See this boy. He is going to be a vindictive man when he grows up. He turned to the guards and said:*

- *Beware this boy. He has all the makings of a warrior.*

Then he let the boy go.

- *And did he run back to the house?*

- No. There was no running. He walked slowly and deliberately back up the hill. I watched him and his face beamed and his eyes glowed. Then he went back to his bed as if nothing had happened.

Ásta looked at the boy, who was playing with Dag, swinging their wooden swords high above their heads.

- And did he say nothing more, the boy?

- I asked him what had happened in the woods. And he told me everything as I have told you. Later, one of the guards saw me with him. He told me to beware of the boy. Apparently, the king had pulled the boy's face close to his and told him that he had passed the first of the trials.

That evening, as they dined together, Ásta, fearing for the safety of her boys, spoke with the King.

- You play too roughly with the boys, Olaf. You reduced them to tears. That's not a brave thing for a mighty king to do – scare his little brothers.

- Were all of them scared, mother?

Ásta ignored the question, telling him instead:

- Please take greater care of them. They will be your heirs one day.

- Perhaps it will not come to that. Astrid...

- Astrid cannot give you an heir, Olaf.

- We shall see, mother. We shall see.

And a smile played on his lips. There were things that his mother didn't know. Things that even a King should keep from his mother. He *would* have a son. But in the meantime, as insurance:

- One of these boys may follow me. But which one?

- It should be Guthorm. He is the eldest.

But the king had stopped listening. Ásta was angry with her oldest son. She wanted nothing more than the surety of knowing that her next-born boy would succeed Olaf and then their lives could continue. Guthorm could join Olaf in the coming years and the two younger boys would run the farms here. But Olaf was playing games. He stood up, pushed the huge carved wooden chair backwards and smiled. It was not a pleasant smile, and Ásta felt the same fear the two boys had felt.

- It should be him who is most worthy of it. I will do my best not to frighten the boys, mother. But there will be other tests.

It was a week later when the king visited the farmstead again. Dag and Harald were taking the runners off the sled and fitting some wheels, helped by one of the farmhands. They were going to use the cart to race against other boys in the town. Halfdán was with the cattle, helping drive them onto the higher ground now that the snow had gone. Guthorm was out with the labourers, sewing seeds for the summer corn. The king's men rounded up the three brothers and told them to meet him on the bridge. The river was swollen and ran fast beneath them. The boys sat on the wooden parapet, dangling their legs, and waited for the king to come. There was a good deal of fear in the air, as they wondered what would happen next. The king kept them waiting. Guthorm and Halfdán found some wooden offcuts dropped from the carts which had collected the felled lumber and taken it back to the village. They sat on the track together and in the mud they drew the shapes of barns and byres. Then they used the wood to build a farmyard, carving some of the bark pieces into animals. They laughed as they carved and shaped their farm.

- What have you built here?

It was the king. He had been watching them as they played.

HARALD HARDRADA - THE LAST VIKING

- It is the farm we shall build when we are older, King Olaf.

- Come, boys. Call me brother. Show me this farm.

And he sat beside them and listened while they showed him. He smiled and nodded as they pointed out its features.

- And where will the farmhouse be?

Guthorm lifted up two square blocks.

- There, brother. One each, at the heart of the farm so that we can see what the men are doing. Keep an eye on them while they work.

The king patted both boys on the head.

- Well done boys. Well done. Kings of the land.

And they smiled at him, and he smiled in return. Then he went down to the river where Harald sat watching as small wooden 'boats' floated down stream, picking up the current.

- So, boy. What game have you devised while you wait for your king?

Harald didn't look up at him. He kept his eyes firmly on the floating wooden pieces.

- These are my warships, King Olaf.'

- Perhaps, kinsman, one day you will have charge of an entire fleet of warships. Perhaps you will lead them into battle.

News had arrived at the town. In King Olaf's absence some of the rebels had ransacked some of the market towns, including Ribe. This was not the first attempt to snatch power and Olaf was planning his journey south, gathering an army to ride and set sail. The summer had almost passed, and before long roads and rivers would become impassable. He had to strike now. He had to assert his power, keep open the trading routes that meant so much to his people. Their last meal together was on a warm, dry evening.

HARALD HARDRADA - THE LAST VIKING

The doors were wide open and cloths drawn back, to get light and air into hall. He had been in Ringerike too long. He had enjoyed the days of peace and feasting. But now he must return to Nidaros where most of his army had camped. But there was something that needed to be settled, for once and for all.

Ásta entered the hall with her five children, and they sat on the bench between their mother and the king. The three boys sat closest to the him.

- *This is my last day for a while. And we have some unfinished business.*

King Olaf moved the boys so that Guthorm and Halfdán sat on either side of him.

- *Now then boys. Your final test. I have a question for each of you. It is this: What would you most like to have?*

Guthorm answered first:

-*That's easy. I want ten farms with fertile lands where I could grow grain every summer. This will make us rich and important.*

Ásta took Guthorm's hand in hers.

- *Unless, son, you become king after your brother.*

Guthorm looked at her.

- *I will always strive to do my duty, mother. As king or farmer.*

The King turned his attention to Halfdán.

- *And what of you, brother? What would you most like to have?*

Halfdán looked across at his brother.

- *For me too this is an easy question my lord. I too would like ten farms, but they will be laden with cattle which will provide milk and meat to all the markets.*

The king nodded.

-*And what of you, young Harald? What would you most like to have?*

HARALD HARDRADA - THE LAST VIKING

Ásta turned to the boy, and Brenn, from her place further down the table, looked at Harald and knew what he would say. His voice was loud and clear:

- *I want loyal warriors, brother.*

Laughter sprang around the table. The king grabbed his hands and lifted him onto the table. Brenn watched him with pride.

- *And how many loyal warriors would make you happy, boy?*

Harald looked down at his brothers.

- *So many that they would eat all of Halfdán's cows, with all of Guthorm's corn. In one meal.*

- *Look after this boy, mother. In him you have brought forth another king.*

Ásta knew better than to argue with her son. His mind was made up. There was time to change it. But for now… the boys were young and perhaps Olaf would take another wife, who would give him a son and heir. Until then, while he was away, she would tutor Guthorm, teach him what he needed to know.

Later, watching Harald and Dag push the cart down the hill, Brenn tried to imagine the future. It had been her milk that had fed the baby boy, alongside Dag at her breast. Would this boy, her charge, be a future king? Brenn's heart glowed with pride. At the bottom of the hill the two boys dragged the cart up again, ready for the next race.

HARALD HARDRADA - THE LAST VIKING

FORAYS

The door was open and she slipped inside. She saw his figure lying on the bed and she watched as he moved himself to a sitting pose. He was beautiful, a young boy but strong and muscular. She pushed the door shut behind her; it groaned and squeaked on its hinges. Then she drew the curtain across the door and the room was sealed.

She approached the bed, watching him watching her. She had heard the stories about this boy. She knew about his strength and his courage, how at the age of ten he had ridden with the king and hunted the wild boar, fearless. She had heard too – all of them had – of his part in the battle by the lake. His blue eyes shone and his long yellow hair hung down to his neck. His hairless chest had beads of sweat glistening, and she could see his narrow hips. She drew near and reached out her hands to him. He took them and allowed her to swing his body round so that he sat, his legs planted on the floor. Then slowly, rhythmically she unhooked the cape and let it fall to the floor, all the time watching him. And he was watching her.

Slowly, she stepped out of her skirts and let them slip so that they too fell about her feet. And all the time his eyes never left her, never for a moment. She took his hands in her own. They were still the hands of a callow youth, smooth and soft. He kept his eyes fixed on her face. His breaths were shorter now. And she felt his back arch and his thighs clench. Then suddenly the release as he came inside her and he lay back on the bed, spent.

She sat there beside him, caressing his chest, his arms, his back, until at last, both of their bodies relaxed and they lay side-by-side on the bed.

HARALD HARDRADA - THE LAST VIKING

In the morning she was gone but the smell and taste of her were on him. He recalled the adventures of the night, saw again her slim white body and felt himself stiffen below. He lay back and wondered if it had all been real, any of it?

His brother, the king, had promised him a gift...
- *A present you will never forget.*
... and he had been true to his word. It was a gift to savour, to remember. He thought about her.

King Olaf had returned to Ringerike to join the celebrations of his thirteenth birthday. He had asked what he wanted most for a present.
- *To go north with you, brother, and root out these rebel farmers.*
- *And what will you do when we find them, little brother?*
- *Use my sword on them. And my axe. Together we shall show this Danish King the way back to his own country.*

King Olaf had laughed at first, but seeing his face, the set of his jaw, realised that this boy was going to be a fearsome ally.
- *Then you shall come. Get yourself ready for a long journey. You will not see your bed again for some months. We shall sleep under the moon and stars, and only return when all their heads are cut off.*

Harald bowed before him, and laid his sword down in front of his brother. Then once the king had dismissed him he ran – briefly a child again – to his chamber, and began to fill a canvas bag. His mother followed him into the room, behind her Brenn.
- *It's not possible, Harald. You are too young still.*
- *My brothers were not too young to take on their farms...*
- *That's different. They were not going into battle.*

HARALD HARDRADA - THE LAST VIKING

- My sisters were both married before they were thirteen.

- That's not the same at all. You know it isn't.

Harald looked beyond his mother towards Brenn. She was smiling. She knew it was useless to argue. The boy had always been the same. Queen Ásta spoke again.

- But what if something happens to you. You could be badly wounded. You could die.

- Then I shall have a place in Valhalla, and you can mourn your son who died a hero's death.

Ásta knew there was little point arguing. The boy had made up his mind. She turned away to hide the tears. She turned back at the doorway before she left. Their eyes locked. This was a battle she could never win. Harald was cut from the same cloth as his brother. The blood that ran through their veins was the same strength. Once his mind was set...

- Then take care of yourself and return here to us in one piece.

Brenn took his canvas bag, emptied it on to the bed.

- Leave this to me, Harald.

She opened the chest in the corner and laid out the clothes he should take.

- It is spring now, and the days will be warm and long. I will pack what you need.

He stood watching her. Brenn had nursed him from a baby; she had looked after him, dressed his wounds when he played too roughly with his older brothers. His boyhood companion had been her son, Dag, and she had watched him grow, taller, fairer and stronger than any of the children.

- Will you let Dag come with me?

Brenn stopped, a tunic held in her hands.

- I would look after him.

- I will talk to him. If he says yes.

HARALD HARDRADA - THE LAST VIKING

- Thank you, Brenn...

And for a moment Brenn saw the little boy nobody else saw: vulnerable; self-doubting.

- ... I will be stronger and braver with Dag by my side.

They had left Ringerike early the next morning. Brenn watched them go. There was dew on the grass, and the sun was already climbing as Harald and Dag rode confidently out of the village, Dag turning to his mother and throwing her a smile, Harald sitting bolt upright riding behind the king. And she watched them go. Further behind, the boy's mother also watched as he rode out. If there were tears in her eyes, she did her best to hide them.

They journeyed north for several days, stopping only to take water and food, which was eaten for sustenance rather than pleasure. The rebels were growing stronger. King Olaf had hoped that each battle would be his last. More than anything else he wanted to settle down and rule his people in peace but there were so many claimants to his throne. He saw no contradiction between the battle he fought and the new religion he had found. Christ had had His battles too, and while he may not have used a sword to beat them, even His hands had been raised against his enemies.

- One last battle, brother. That's all we must fight. Then when they are defeated I will settle for a quiet life. Perhaps I shall even let you rule in my place.

- I am not ready to be king, Olaf. But I am ready to fight for one.

And he waved his sword high over his head. Riding behind his brother, he felt every inch the warrior. He hadn't yet had to prove himself but when his time came he knew he would be ready. He swung round in the saddle and waved the sword at Dag, some way back with the rest of the Kings-guard. Even from this distance he could see his friend's smile, wide and toothy. Together they would fight the tyranny of Danish King Cnut, and stop him driving the true Norwegian army into the sea.

King Olaf joined his army at Stikelstad. The camp was huge, spread out between the river and the mighty lake. The mountains protected them from the north and the woods spread down to the river. The soldiers had cut down part of the wood so that they had a clear view and could not be surprised. Most had journeyed to the camp on board their mighty ships and, with the fallen trees, other craft were being made. They had been laid out alongside the harbour the troops had dug out. They were almost ready for battle. The king had planned an assault from river and land. Harald and Dag spent the first night resting. Dag slept under the upturned boats alongside the river, while Harald joined the king's bodyguard in the temporary wooden structure that was dining hall and bedchamber as well as a strategic headquarters. In the morning, Harald joined the warriors at the huge table on which sat models of ships and trees and mountains, drawn up like some giant chess game. He hung back from the conversation, chewing on the bread and sipping from the ale-cup. He watched his brother, his king, as he listened to his captains; watched as he moved pieces on the board; watched as he reached his decisions and then sent them out to relay their orders. Olaf turned to Harald.

- Well, little brother, what do you make of it all?

- War is a mighty game, my lord. And it is played best by those who listen as well as talk.

HARALD HARDRADA - THE LAST VIKING

And Olaf slapped him on the back and laughed.

- *So, little brother, you are learning fast.*

They were interrupted by a soldier who made his way to the king, and whispered in his ear.

- *Come with me, Harald. We have a report of a raiding party, who have come to chip away at our army. Collect that friend of yours and prepare to ride out to meet them.* Harald looked at him, and his brother read his face. Only Brenn and Dag had been able to tell what he was thinking. Now it seemed the king could do so too.

- *There's no better way to find out if you are ready than to do the thing, Harald. Go. Fetch Dag. Saddle up and meet me by the harbour.*

Harald drank the ale to the dregs, finished the bread and went in search of his friend.

The king's men had chased the rebels northward, along the lake shore. There they trapped them and though they fought bravely the rebels were driven back into the sea. It was Harald's first kill. He had slashed at the rebel's neck and watched the blood spurt high into the air. He felt the warmth of it on his face. Then he roared as he chased the rest of them down to the water's edge. One of them, their leader, was captured and taken back. It was Dag who had held the wounded man on the end of his drawn dagger, until others came to take him away. Back at the camp they questioned him, torturing the answers from him.

- *This man has served his purpose. We shall send his head back in a bag for the rest of his fellows to see their own fate.*

He was taken, dragged across the stony ground, to a makeshift block. There his head was placed on the stump of an old tree. The king handed an axe to Harald.

30

HARALD HARDRADA - THE LAST VIKING

- When we go hunting for boar, little brother, it is the newest and youngest hunters that are bloodied with the hot blood of the wild creature. I have seen you fight like a soldier today with blood on your face. Now can you do this? Chop off a man's head?

Harald looked at his king. He said nothing, just held out his hand. The king passed him the axe.

- Take a mighty swing, little brother. No man should have to survive two blows to the neck.

Harald looked at the rebel. He was past saving. The torturers had done their work on him and his body was already broken. This blow would come as a relief to him. He raised the axe, high above his head and brought it down with all his strength in one rhythmical stroke. He heard the crack of bone as the head juddered. But it stayed still, and the eyes still moved. They pleaded for death. Harald swung the axe again and watched as the head rolled. The eyes closed, the body rolled backwards and the stump was covered in blood.

- That will send them home, at least for a while. A leaderless army is no army at all.

Ten days after the skirmish by the lake, the king led a large army down river. Harald had stayed at the camp.

- A king and his heir must be separated in battle, little brother. You must remain here.

He saw the look on Harald's face. He almost gave in to it.

- You will stay here. I shall return soon and then we shall have much to celebrate.

And they had gone, leaving a small guard to keep watch over the camp. The days passed slowly and they amused themselves by hunting in the woods. Many a boar was slain and hung to be butchered, ready for a king's feast. And at night, after the drinking and singing which he happily joined in, he heard the rustling in the camp as women passed in and out of the men's quarters. Harald lay awake and listened to the noises. It was a new world. A world of battle. A world where men were warriors by day and lovers by night. And it was still strange to him.

When the army returned, when the boats had all been moored, the King came to him and promised him a gift.

The summer had almost passed when Brenn saw the two of them riding through the meadows. News of them had arrived during the months they'd been away, but between each message Brenn feared the worst. She feared more for the boy than she did for her own son. She knew that so long as Harald were alive, Dag would be safe. So she swept the floors, emptied the cesspits and shovelled the shit into the pigsties. And occasionally she would stop, put her hand to her eyes and look for them coming. The nights already outmatched the days, and the cold winds had arrived when she caught sight of the two of them, racing towards the village.

She sent the girl who was helping her spread the filthy muck to fetch her mistress. By the time they had drawn level with her, Harald just ahead of the race, Ásta was standing next to her.

- *Our sons have come home, Brenn. Pour them ale, fetch them some meat. They must be weary.*

But Brenn hung back until she saw them both dismount, until their feet were on solid ground. Dag came to see him much later, after they had eaten, and after they had washed their bodies. His normally unlined face was creased.

- There is news of Gunnhild. Your sister is ill.

Harald spoke with Brenn. There were stories, she told him, of how her husband beat her.

- I don't know the truth of it, but he is not a good man.

- I shall go tomorrow, and pay them a visit.

Gunnhild lived a mile or so from the village, and at daybreak, while the ground was still wet and the air cold, Harald walked to the farmhouse that was his sister's home. As he approached the house he heard shouting, and Gunnhild ran from the house. At the sight of her brother she stopped, and held out her hands to him.

- Harald. When did you return to us?

- Yesterday, sister. I have heard that you are not well.

Behind her, in the doorway, stood her husband, a tall stocky man, ruddy faced and big-shouldered. He held a belt in his hand and the buckle hung down.

- What do you want, Harald? Why are you on my land?

Harald looked at the swinging buckle, then at his sister's face. He saw the blood on her arm and her chest. He smelt the fear in the air. It reminded him of the battlefield. He said nothing but stood watching the man and his swinging buckle.

- Get off my land or I shall give you the same.

And the farmer swung the buckle like a sling.

Harald felt his fists clench.

- I have come to fetch my sister home. Where I can look after her.

He saw Gunnhild's eyes moving, heard the terror in her voice.

- You will make things worse for me, Harald. It is good to see you home safe, but leave now. I shall be fine.

The farmer took a step towards him.

HARALD HARDRADA - THE LAST VIKING

- If you come again, I shall set the dog on you, boy.

Harald took a last look at his sister then turned away, his fists still at his side.

- I shall come back for you, Gunnhild.

They both watched him go. Then she turned back to the farmhouse. He raised the strap and she screamed as the buckle hit her across the chest. Harald heard his sister scream, and the noise stayed in his head all the way back to his home.

It was dark when he returned. He strapped the axe on his back and wound the rope round his body. The path to the farm was rutted but hard and in the moonlight it was easy to see where to put his feet. Ahead of him he heard the screams of his sister and he could feel his blood boiling in his veins. His heart was pumping fast, and he remembered his fight at the lake. Suddenly the dog was on him, snarling and biting. He kicked out, and managed to pull his axe clear. As the dog jumped for his throat, he swung the axe and it fell dead. He swung the axe again; he wouldn't need two swings this time. He grabbed the dog's head, dripping blood on his clothes. He uncoiled the rope and went into the house. His sister lay on the floor. There was blood coming from her face. Beyond lay the bedchamber, and Harald grabbed a pot that hung above the stove and marched in. He threw the dog's head onto the bed. The farmer jumped up and ran at the boy with fists flailing. Harald side-stepped the lunge and swung the pot. The noise of metal on bone echoed through the farmhouse.

He tied the rope around the man's neck and hauled him to his feet, pulling him out of the door to a barn. He heard the animals shuffling as he pulled the struggling farmer through into the middle. He swung the end of the rope over a wooden beam that stretched from one end of the barn to the other, catching the free end. Then he pulled it. At first the farmer barely moved but

HARALD HARDRADA - THE LAST VIKING

gradually his feet left the floor and he was hanging above the straw-covered earth. The farmer hung there, his hands trying with all the strength he had to pull the rope clear of his neck. But his weight was killing him. Harald let the rope drop and the farmer fell to the floor lying in a terrified heap. The hot stench of shit and piss filled the air and Harald stood astride him.

- My sister is coming back home. Thank the gods I spared your life.
And together Gunnhild and Harald returned home. It was Brenn, looking out into the darkness that saw them return together and she smiled. It was good to have the boy back.

HARALD HARDRADA - THE LAST VIKING

HEIRS

Brenn was worried.

She watched as the boy grew. Side by side with Dag he worked the fields of his mother's farm, every day until the sun was setting. Then he and Dag would sharpen their swords and spar, the sound of metal on metal jarring long into the night. She knew the signs. She had watched other young men grow restless and long for the battlegrounds. What news they got from the king was scarce, and made bad reading. Each time the rider appeared, his cloak torn, his face bloodied, the news was worse. They feared for their lives. King Cnut, the Dane who now ruled over them all, was fighting against the Norwegian patriots trying to recapture their beloved country led by Olaf who was trying hard to free their country of his tyranny. Harald was fretting. He was waiting to be called by his brother; waiting for his chance to bear a sword and shield in the name of freedom. And Brenn knew when that day came, both of the boys would go. Boys! She always thought of them as boys, but they were men now, sporting wispy beards and drinking ale into the early morning. And that wasn't all. Harald and Dag were no strangers to the beds of the young women who hung around the farmstead.

She saw the dust rising in the distance, dust being kicked up by the hooves of a fast-ridden horse. More news from the king. It would not be good. Brenn hung around the entrance to the Big House, and waited until the rider's horse was tethered and watered. She saw the boys come running from the fields, drawn by the flying hooves, eager for news of battle. By the time they had arrived at Brenn's side, the rider was knelt before the king's mother.

- *My Lady Ásta.*

HARALD HARDRADA - THE LAST VIKING

- What news from your lord?

- Olaf is in retreat, My Lady.

- Retreat? Is he beaten? Is Cnut's army riding down upon us like a wolf, to slaughter these lambs?

- My lord Olaf has set up his camp again at Stikelstad. They say it will be the final battle.

Harald pushed his way into the hallway. There was no-one bold enough to stop him.

- We are not lambs, mother. Let the Danish soldiers come and they shall find us like lions, ready to tear at their throats. Attend to this man. Get him food and drink. Mend his wounds.

Harald raised the rider to his feet.

- I shall return with you to my brother's camp. If there is to be a final battle, then I shall be at his side. Together we shall drive back the Danish king, drive him into the sea, so that the water will turn red all the way to his England. This usurper will see what sort of men he is dealing with.

Brenn watched him, and she watched too her own son, Dag. She knew he would go with Harald. They were not to be separated, the two of them. The rider was being led away, for food and comfort, but hearing the boy speak he turned.

- I must return. As soon as my horse is ready, I must return. For our true king has need of every man.

When the rider was dismissed, Ásta beckoned to her youngest son.

- If your brother is to die, you, as his heir, must be far away. You must be ready to inherit...

- I am not his heir, mother. You know that. Magnus will inherit.

- Magnus is a bastard boy. He is not the true heir.

They all knew. It was common knowledge. Frustrated by his wife's inability to bear a live child, Olaf had sought an heir elsewhere. And Alfhild, a servant in his wife's entourage had given him what he most desired. A boy heir. Magnus. They all knew too that the three of them had fled, seeking help wherever they could. Magnus was, by all accounts a sickly child, not expected to live long. Then, when the Swedish King had given them a ship, the remnants of the army sailed back to Norway. Nobody had known exactly where Olaf was. He, Magnus and his mother disappeared. It was two years later that Olaf emerged from hiding, leading a small army to claim back the throne he'd lost.

- *There will be nothing to inherit, mother, if my brother loses this battle. What difference will it make if I am with him or not?*

- *It will make a difference if you are killed. What then will happen to our line?*

- *There are my two brothers. They will follow on.*

Ásta took his hand. Then she pushed his long hair back behind his ears.

- *They are not made for fighting. They are farmers. They are good farmers but they will make poor kings. No. Norway's future may lie in your hands. Therefore, you must not return to fight this battle. Instead go south. Flee to warmer lands, out of the reach of Denmark. Then in better times you can return and take back what is rightfully yours.*

But she knew there was no point in her words. His ears were closed to any sound other than those of battle. It was his destiny to fight alongside Olaf. She knew it but she must try.

- *Olaf himself will not allow it. The king will forbid it.*

Harald moved back, away from his mother, so that her hands fell to her side.

- *Then let my brother himself tell me so. For I shall listen to no other.*

He turned away from his mother and sought out the rider.

HARALD HARDRADA - THE LAST VIKING

- Come, sir. When you are ready, I shall return with you. And there
will be tribute too. The village has already collected money to help
raise a large army, and we shall find more now to keep them fed.

As he passed her, standing in the doorway, Brenn took his hand.
The boy looked at her.

- Will you take Dag too?

- Does he want to come to war, Brenn?

- He will follow you to the very edge of Hell. He will follow you with
every ounce of his strength.

- Then I shall take him.

- And you will look out for him?

- If he will look out for me.

And Brenn took his hands in hers and kissed them. He felt the
warm tears there too. Brenn feared this would be the last time
she saw her son. But she knew too that she would not have the
power to stop Dag following his boyhood friend into the battle.

- I shall bring him back safe to you, Brenn. I shall watch over him,
as you have always watched over me.

And the next morning, with the sun starting to rise, Brenn watched
as her two boys left the village and rode north. They were armed
for battle.

They arrived the next day just as the sun was highest in the sky.
Their heavy horses had made slow progress. They had rested
overnight in a wooded glen, close by the outspread finger of a
fjord, bathing in the cold waters. Then before the sun was above
the horizon the three set off again, the rider leading the way. They
had smelt the sea before they arrived at the camp and they
descended the hill watching the camp grow as they rode nearer.

HARALD HARDRADA - THE LAST VIKING

The Danish ships were off in the distance, not so different from their own. The prows seemed less tall, less fearsome than their own, but seeing them there, a fleet of them drawn up, Harald knew this would be a battle. He handed the horses to one of the sentinels and sent Dag away to the soldier's camp.

- Be sure to get plenty to eat, Dag. We shall need all of our strength today.

King Olaf welcomed him, arms wide, a smile on his face. But Harald saw signs of fatigue and scars of battle on his brother's face.

-Welcome, little brother. So you have come to fulfil your destiny, have you?

- I have come to join the battle for Norway, King Olaf.

- You may well be its king yourself, little brother, before the night is done.

- You shall still be king, brother, when we send Cnut home.

Olaf led him to a sheltered quiet spot in the woods that lay on the edge of the camp. Around him, men were chopping down trees to broaden the open land. Against the sound of axes and falling trees, his brother spoke to him, where none could overhear them.

- I am not afraid to die, Harald. This will be a hard-fought battle, for Cnut is determined to break us once and for all.

- I am proud to stand alongside you brother, and fight with all my strength. Together we will not be beaten.

- I am not afraid to die, but I am afraid that we should die together.

Harald wanted to answer his brother but the king held up his hand.

- I think it better that my brother should not take part in the battle.

- You think me still a child.

- You are still a child.

- I have seen fifteen years. I have a beard. I have a strong arm.

40

HARALD HARDRADA - THE LAST VIKING

- But you are still a boy, Harald, and a boy who must be ready to succeed me in Norway if I fall today.

Harald turned away from his brother. He didn't want to let the King see the tears in his eyes. They were hot on his face. They were tears of anger. He wiped them on his sleeve as he turned back.

- I shall certainly take part in this battle.

This time he held his hand up to silence the king.

- And if I am too weak to grip my sword, I know what to do.

Harald pulled some rope from the pocket of his tunic and wrapped it around his sword and his wrist.

- I shall tie this hand to the hilt. These farmers who fight for the Dane... There is no-one more eager, and no-one better alive than I to cause trouble for these farmers.

Harald drew an arc with his arm indicating the camp of loyal soldiers.

- I intend to be with my men.

King Olaf took his arm. They stood locked together in defiance.

The king returned to the men, Harald alongside him. They made their way through the camp. At each knot of soldiers, Olaf spoke with the men, and they smiled, lifting their whetstones off their gleaming swords. At the very centre stood a rampart of shields, each one richly adorned. There, inside this defensive ring the king called his skalds to him, the poets whose job it was to record the deeds of warrior kings; the annalists of the court.

- You are to stay here and see what happens; then you will not need others to tell you of it later, for you can tell the story and make verses about it yourselves afterwards.

Amongst them, Harald recognised Thorkel Skallason. It was his poetry that had been recited by the heralds who came to the village to tell of the mighty King Olaf. It was his words that led to

HARALD HARDRADA - THE LAST VIKING

Olaf's reputation as a good king. And now Harald stood alongside this skald, and others like him. Skallason's voice was deep and rich. He stood stock still and spoke his words.

> *All Kings have to be brave, gallant in battle, and*
> *scourges of their enemies. King Olaf, the Second of*
> *that name was such a King, and shall be again. We,*
> *your skalds, will sing your praises and tell of your*
> *great victory today and forever people will sing of*
> *the Battle of Stikelstad. And they will be recorded*
> *for all time in the runes that we carve today.*

When they heard the shouts of the invading horde, they ran together back to the head of the army. There they stood, and waited. Swords drawn, shields held before them, waiting for the blood to run. The sun was still high in the sky. It felt warm on their faces as they waited for whatever would follow. The Peasant Army marched towards them, their makeshift weapons drawn, and their voices filling the air with fearful screams. And in Ringerike, far to the south, Brenn thought she heard those screams and her tears fell.

The farmer watched from his hiding place on the hill. He saw the young soldiers, two of them together, walking through the field of bodies. The dead littered the ground from the hill to the shores. Cnut's ships still sat in the fjord, and his soldiers were loading dead men's weapons onto them.

He watched as the two wounded soldiers picked their way across muddy fields stained red with Norwegian blood. Dead soldiers, dead oxen, dead horses, carcases which had ceased twitching in their final throes, eyes open to the evening sun, limbs twisted, guts torn out and strewn.

He watched as they climbed the hill, watched from above. He watched as they moved between the bodies. One of them, taller with long hair that was matted with blood, limped, and held his side, from where blood oozed. The other held him upright.

He had seen it all, this peasant farmer. He'd followed the True King into battle; followed though they were all doomed to die a bloody death. He'd run when there was nothing else a man could do, and lay down and watched. Wave after wave of Cnut's men came, butchering all in their path until finally Olaf himself fell, under the force of ten soldiers upon him. But they were not Cnut's soldiers who had slain him. They were his own men. None of it made any sense to the farmer, who still watched until finally the battle ceased and Cnut marched back to his ships. The great battle of Stikelstad was over, and the True King lay dead. He watched the two soldiers as they crested the hill, and they sat together looking back down on the carnage. As he crept towards them, the sounds deadened by the bracken, they suddenly looked at him. They hadn't heard him. They had sensed his presence. He raised his head, and the taller of the two lifted his sword.

- *We have seen you. We know you are there. Show yourself or you will die where you lie.*

He lifted his head, and then his hands. The farmer had no sword. He had never owned a sword. All his fighting had been done with bill-hook and sickle. It was the taller one who spoke again.

- *Stand up. Stand where we can see you.*

He stood. Still. He waited for them to rush on him. He had survived the battle. Would he now die from the swords of men from his own side? If they could kill their own leader, what hope was there for him? A peasant. A farmer's son. A louse. A nothing.

HARALD HARDRADA - THE LAST VIKING

But there was no rush. The men stood and the raised swords dropped to their sides. The other man, the shorter, swarthier one, spoke:

- *We must go. There will be a time to settle scores, but the wise thing now is to run.*
- *And when did Dag get to be so wise?*
- *When his companion was so foolish.*

The peasant watched, still afraid, still unsure of what they would do.

- *If you two men will follow me. I know this land. My father has farmed here for years and his father before him. There are hiding places. Places where you can rest, where you can be tended, and wounds mended. Follow me.*
- *What is your name? How do we know you are not leading us into danger?*
- *I am nobody, just a farmer. Names are not important now.*

And he turned away from them. He was still nervous. What would they do? But he had survived this far. Survived the battle. Surely he wasn't destined to die now that it was over. He heard them following behind.

They were still walking long after night had fallen. They put as much distance between themselves and the bloody fields as they could. But progress was slow, and the wounded man's blood dripped a trail behind them. The tall fair-haired youth grew weaker.

When he had first seen them, the peasant hadn't noticed anything about these men other than their swords and the blood-spattered clothing. But now he realised they were both young. Neither had reached half his age. At one of their increasingly frequent rests, the tall one asked:

HARALD HARDRADA - THE LAST VIKING

- Where are we heading? Where are you taking us? Is it a trap? Are you true man or traitor?

And he had told them. Angry.

- I am no traitor. It was not I who took my own True King's life. I fought beside him against Cnut.

- What do you mean? We all fought alongside Olaf.

- Not all.

And he told them what he'd seen. Told them of the traitorous blows thrust into Olaf's body. And the two young men listened in silence. And he watched as the taller, long-haired youth brooded on the news. They set off again and just as the sun was rising they reached the farmhouse. It was quiet and still, but all three sensed they were being watched. A few yards from the doorway, the farmer waved his hands high above his head.

- I have brave soldiers with me, who need our help.

Suddenly they were surrounded by women. The fair-haired soldier fell into the arms of an older woman who had run to them. He closed his eyes and allowed himself to be carried inside the farmhouse. And there, with Dag beside him, Harald slept. And only Dag knew who the wounded soldier was.

And far off to the south, Brenn held her breath, waiting for the boy to waken. She had no idea where they were but she sensed they were both alive, however unlikely that seemed. News from the battle had reached them. Ásta had received the small group of men who had come back to tell the Queen their story of her son's death. They had with them carved in runes, the words of Olaf's skald, written on his own deathbed. Skallason's voice sounded from the grave:

HARALD HARDRADA - THE LAST VIKING

I saw the hail of arrows
That raged around the King,
And I saw the younger brother
A boy of just fifteen.
When on the field of battle,
King Olaf's body slain,
The boy fled to a secret place;
Their battle all in vain.

She had lost Olaf, but it seemed that Harald was still alive. Brenn didn't need to hear the words. She already knew. Both her boys were alive. Somewhere out there.

Three days had come and gone before he opened his eyes. The room was smoky and full of people who watched him. Next to his bed was Dag. His body felt weak, and the pain under his ribs was acute. But his clothes were fresh and a girl came with broth, thin but scalding hot. Later, when they thought they had the smoky room to themselves, when the only light came from the full moon which shone through the open window, he raised himself and talked in whispers to Dag. From his shadowed corner the farmer's son listened.

- *Once I am healed, we must raise an army. We must hunt down Cnut. We must avenge my brother.*

Dag looked at his friend, his eyes shining, reflecting the white moon. It was the farmer's voice they heard.

- *We must leave the fight to others. You must leave Norway, for now, until the times are changed. When the King's son, Magnus returns to us, we can raise an army and win our country back. I have had word from Earl Brusason. There are others, loyal to*

HARALD HARDRADA - THE LAST VIKING

*Norway, who will meet us beyond the mountains and he will meet
us there.*

Dag asked:

- And what news of Magnus? What news of the King's heir?

There was none. The young prince had disappeared. Harald had
never seen the boy. This bastard had no rights to his claim. But
that would wait. Perhaps Magnus was gone forever. In which
case, he, Harald, was Olaf's chosen heir.

He sank back onto his bed with a wince. He hated to admit the
farmer was right. Run today; rebuild an army and return for the
fight tomorrow. Let them all believe that he, Olaf's brother, true
heir to Norway was dead with the rest of Olaf's army. If what he
had heard was true, there were still spies and traitors about who
wanted him dead. If they *had* killed his brother what would stop
them hunting him down once his body was not found among the
dead. The farmer spoke again, before leaving them alone:

*- We shall set off again tomorrow heading south. In two weeks, we
shall cross the Kjolen Mountains. And then we shall go east.*

They set out early, kept clear of the main tracks, the traders'
routes, where spices and silks were transported. They slept in the
cover of the forest at night and gradually the young warrior
regained his strength and he and his companion walked side by
side following some distance behind the farmer. He would stop
soon and let them catch up. It was obvious from the way he
walked that the boy's ribs and leg were still sore but he was
getting stronger. He would live to fight another day. The two of
them were clearly close friends. They talked about their families

and their home far to the south-west. He heard little of what they said. His eyes were constantly on the lookout for danger.

Behind him, Harald grew in confidence. He had regained that sense of himself, of his destiny. Dag recognised again the boy he had known all his life. With his lust for fame and glory.

- For now, I go creeping from forest to forest with little honour. Who knows? Perhaps my name may yet become renowned far and wide... in the end.

The boy had returned.

HARALD HARDRADA - THE LAST VIKING
DAG

Winter followed them southward. Green hills in the distance became snowy uplands as they drew near. By the time they reached them and started the climb their boots trudged through newly-fallen snow. The air was colder despite their southern progress. The days had been divided between riding the heavy horses - with their hairy fetlocks and thick manes, their coats adapting to the cold – and progress on foot, leading the huge but gentle beasts ever forward. As the miles passed, Dag saw the change in his boyhood friend.

- I have lost more than a battle at Stikelstad, I have lost a kingdom. With my brother's death, my claim to the kingdom died too.

Dag took him to one side, allowing the farmer to draw further out of earshot.

- There are still many of us, who will fight to see you crowned the true king. But for now we must let Cnut have his victory. It is a battle we lost, not a war. You are our country's hope. Our best chance of independence. You will come back and shake off the yoke of the Danish king. Magnus has disappeared. You will return.

All along the route they had talked about the rumours they had heard. As they passed through villages, empty of men, the women talked of treachery against Olaf. The dead king's name name was held in high esteem among these farmers. Some had built churches, following his lead, turning away from the old ways. But they had heard that Harald the half-brother, had betrayed him in battle and they cursed out loud and spat at the traitors' deeds. And in their minds, Harald, the half-brother was the guilty man. Only later when the poets' stories were heard and committed to memory, did the old tales die and new stories of bravery and heroism emerge. Olaf was a saint, a great king, and Harald his worthy thane. But here in the hillside farms the women welcomed the three unknown men into their homes, gave them shelter, not knowing who they were. The farmer told the story of how he'd found them wandering out of the battle, bloodied, wounded and defeated. He had told the two soldiers he led onward that there was a meeting planned – a Great Moot – which would be presided over by Earl Rognvald Brusason. He was certain that there would be many fugitives there, waiting for them, in Sweden, under the protection of the Rus Grand Duke. The earl was preparing an army to put Magnus on the throne. They had taken the news many miles with them and Dag watched his friend chew over the words.

- So it has all been for Magnus. For the bastard boy we have risked our lives.

And Dag listened while Harald talked of Esau and his lost birthright, a story he knew vaguely from his days in the classroom. They sat together in the candlelit cottage, and Dag listened to Harald, whispering in the dark.

- I'll not fight to put the boy onto the throne of Norway. Magnus has more need of me than I of him.

And Harald flexed his arm, and gripped the sword. He had grown stronger with each day and he was a force again.

- No, Dag. I will not fight yet. Besides, Cnut is too strong still. There will be a better time to return to battle.

Dag had seen this change in him. He thought like a general now, not a soldier. He talked about tactics and plans. He had learned much, this boy.

That night two of the young girls who worked on the farm came to them and warmed their beds. Dag was inexperienced but the girl showed him how to give her, and himself pleasure. And as he lay back, he heard the moans from his friend's bunk, and knew that Harald was a more experienced lover. Before sunrise the girls had gone, probably into the fields, to bring the sheep and cattle into the warm barns, where the wind bit less furiously. They were on the road early again, the three of them, riding slowly through the snow, the warm-bodied girls already a distant memory. The two men kept themselves apart from the farmer who led them through the passes.

- I'll not stay to fight with Cnut. Let him have his victory for now. He will not live to be an old man. I will go east. There are countries I have heard of, where they will welcome two brave soldiers with arms that are strong and swords that are sharp. What about it Dag?

And Dag nodded. But he had also heard of these foreign lands and preferred the comforts of home. But he would not leave his friend and lord. He had made a promise to his mother. And far away Brenn knew her son and the boy were safe.

- And perhaps while we are there we shall make our fortunes?

- Returning rich men, Dag. Rich and powerful.

Days passed. Weeks passed. Winter came and held up their progress and then in spring they continued, stronger, sporting long hair and beards. Dag and Harald and the farmer who led them. They were heading eastward now, blinded by the low morning sun. The villages grew more numerous and green shoots gave colour and life to the farms they passed. And when they stopped, the only men to be seen there in a year, they ate, drank and slept with the women who were as much in need of company as they were. Word spread of the handsome strangers, often arriving before they themselves arrived, for they kept to the side tracks, through the burgeoning woods, filling with leaves and breaking into blossom. They were close to the borders now. They had been joined by a small group of Swedish men, who would bring them safely into their country. As they came, so the farmer left:

- *To return home. To my wife and my three boys. But we shall wait your return, soldiers. We shall follow you and the king's son back into battle.*

The two soldiers hugged him warmly. It was the taller of the two who bade him goodbye:

- *We shall not forget the service you have done here. We shall have need of you and your boys when we return with the rightful king.*

Harald meant his own rights. And the peasant smiled and thought he meant Magnus. The farmer left them, when the Earl's men found them. The Earl was awaiting them.

It was impossible to tell when they passed from Norway into Sweden, but Dag and Harald sensed they were in a different place. They noticed first that the fields were better tended. There were men in the villages and it was only the unmarried daughters who came to see them at night, and their lovemaking was more vigorous, noisier. There was more food. Wild boar was caught and roasted on a spit, turned by young boys. There was more laughter. There was more life. And as they left the villages, they were followed for a mile or more by the girls and their laughter.

HARALD HARDRADA - THE LAST VIKING

Eventually, almost a year after the Great Battle, they came before Earl Rognvald Brusason. There was no hiding the truth now. He knew Harald by sight, and greeted him by his own name.

- Welcome Harald Sigurdsson. We have heard news of your coming. You were brother of a king, and soon you shall be uncle of a king. We shall plan together for the return of Olaf's line to the throne of Norway.

Harald stayed silent. Dag had gone to join the other soldiers who had escaped the battle. There were more than he had expected. They had all fled to Sweden and now lived lives as exiles. Harald sat at the table alongside the earl, who stood to address the others around the table set up in the Moot Hall. He made no reply to the welcome, merely sat and listened to the plans.

- Stikelstad is our history. King Olaf is dead and we mourn his passing. He was a great king and a wise one, and we all mourn his loss. But now it is to the future we look. To Magnus, the king's son...

- The bastard prince, Harald said under his breath. Brusason continued.

- The Prince is in hiding. He is safe with his mother...

(- Alfhild the Slave)

- ... He is protected by Gracious Sweden to whose mercy they fled after his father lost his Kingdom. The boy knows his father is dead. He knows his time will come. As yet he is just six years old, but he will grow into a fine and strong king. I have met the boy. He will be a worthy heir to Norway.

(- Over my dead body)

- But these are bad times for those of us who love our country. Cnut stands astride us, a bloody tyrant, but he has stretched himself too far. He will face rebellions across his empire. The Angles across to the East love him no more than we do. And we

shall wait. We shall play the long game. When Magnus is ready, when Norway is ready we shall return to free our countrymen. We shall return to fight again. And we shall take skalds with us to write of our deeds, and they will be heralded throughout time.

The Earl's speech had the desired effect. Cups were raised and emptied; and more ale was called for. By the end of the night the hall was full of sleeping, snoring men. All but two. Harald watched them all alongside the Earl.

- *Let them sleep, Harald. They have journeyed far to be here.*

- *And what of me, Rognvald? What is my place in these schemes of yours?*

- *I have two ships waiting. In two days, we shall fill them with fighting men and victuals, and you shall make your way eastward to the court of Jaroslav, Grand Duke of the Rus. Keep your identity secret, you are sought out by the spies of Cnut. You shall travel with my son, Eilif. Jaroslav has heard of your prowess, and the two of you will lead his Viking army.*

- *He will welcome us?*

- *It is certain. You are promised leadership of armies. Jaroslav has his battles to fight. Slavs and Poles seek to break his Empire. In his name, we shall make conquests. We shall gather alliances...*

- *Shall we make money?*

- *Lots of money, Harald. But now it is time for bed. I have a room for you befitting a king's uncle.*

Harald smiled to himself and to the earl's retreating back he said:

- *I'd rather have one fit for a king.*

His lovemaking that night was angry and cruel. The young servant had seemed willing enough but when he turned her on her front and made thrust after thrust inside her, she screamed out. He put his hand over her mouth and continued inside her until he could give no more. She crept away from the bedroom sore and bloodied while his snores filled the room.

In the morning he went to find Dag.

- Have you heard the plans? Jaroslav is sending us out to lead the Rus Vikings. That is our destiny, Dag. To be great leaders of Viking men.

- I know what you are destined to do.

- You too will become a rich man, working for this foreign duke.

- Not me, Harald. I'll not sail with you. I'll return home. My promise is fulfilled.

Harald looked at him; only Dag would dare to cross him. He took him in a huge embrace and then let him go. And away to the west, Brenn felt her heart slow. Her son was coming home, but the boy was moving on. She told Ásta, and the old Queen mourned the loss of another son.

The constant flow of men to and from the ships occupied Harald's time. He was responsible for checking the armoury. Swords had to be sharpened and shields polished so that the sun reflected in their enemy's faces. Other weapons were tested and inspected: axes, hammers, maces. They were loaded into huge chests and carried by eight men onto the ships. The sails were checked, patched where they needed to be, and masts erected. On his last day in Norway, Harald and Dag parted. A quiet dignified grasp of the arm this time. There had been words enough, and now was the time for both men to fulfil their destinies. One would return to his farm back in Ringerike, the other would leave his homeland for many years. Neither had spent time apart in so many years. But there were no tears. Harald watched him leave, two horses laden with food for the journey. As the dust settled he called out to the retreating Dag,

- Take my heart with you back to Brenn, and to my mother. I will return to Norway when I can.

And Dag raised his hand in a final salute.

> *From your avaricious sword you wiped*
> *The blood of fallen men.*
> *Bodies left upon the fields*
> *To be food for black raven.*
> *And so sweet prince, warrior king,*
> *You fled eastward to the Rus;*
> *Nowhere has there ever been*
> *A man more brave than you.*

1066

HARALD HARDRADA - THE LAST VIKING

THE RIVER OUSE AT SELBY. We arrive at our first real town. Our first English town, with its ferry so that citizens on both sides can meet and trade freely. The absence of bridges has been to our advantage, enabling us to sail upriver without hauling the boats round. The taxes are waived when they see the King.

Our army is swelled; growing larger with each village we pass. Here in Selby there are smiths who are busy at their forges, making weapons for this ragtag army. Farmers and butchers set aside their scythes and cleavers and take hold of their new swords and shields, wielding them as though they were still implements of work rather than weapons of war. The king's army is marching alongside the ships as they sail further north. They chatter as they march, a constant sea of sound, accompanied, especially at night, by strange songs and unusual instruments – air-filled pigs' bladders held under their arms with pipes sticking out in all directions. And what a noise. Enough to scare any forces they encounter, but as yet they are untried. Nowhere do we meet resistance. This is Viking land and these are Viking men, no matter their Angle features. And the women welcome us too, opening their skirts and their legs to give succour to hungry sailors; all part of the war effort. It was a patriotic act to warm the beds of the Viking liberators.

I stay aboard, preferring to watch from a distance. Once again the king is surrounded, a great wide circle of admirers: soldiers who will follow him to the ends of the earth, or certainly to Jorvik; soldiers who swear their allegiance with every cup of mead. And there are many cups drunk. Then Tostig Godwinson arrives. We know he is the brother of King Harold, the usurper king, so we are wary of him and his men. But Harald greets him warmly and tells these homespun soldiers that he will lead them to fight their

HARALD HARDRADA - THE LAST VIKING

leader's brother's army. And in the reflected light of King Harald, Tostig too is toasted and cheered. Harald speaks to the men, telling us all of the approaching battle. We will face the English soldiers led by Edwin of Mercia. And he promises us victory. And Harald and Tostig embrace, to wild cheering.

And I watch from the ship, wondering how many of us will survive the battle. From the town stores, we replenish our food and water supplies. Later the King appoints captains to lead the army northwards. The army smells blood, and sharpened swords and painted shields glint in the watery sunlight.

Harald orders the sails to be raised.

1031 - 1038

With swords together,
Two warriors fought;
Shield to shield,
Their men aligned.
To rebellious Slavs
Scant mercy shown;
The warring Poles
Driven home.

HARALD HARDRADA - THE LAST VIKING
WISDOM

Harald set sail, almost a year to the day after he'd arrived on the coast of Sweden. The news of Ásta's death had darkened his mood. He mourned her loss, and he regretted the distance that fate had put between them. It had been some years since he had seen his mother. He hoped she was watching him now as he set out to fulfil his destiny. Now he was headed for the land of Kiev Rus. Three years after Olaf had sought sanctuary there, when Cnut conquered Norway, his youngest brother Harald set sail, seeking the shelter and patronage of Grand Duke Jaroslav. He went with other Norwegians who had made their way over the mountains and across Sweden, all men who looked forward to a time they could return to their own country, ruled by one of their own. Magnus was the hope, the boy king that would free them all. Until then they would look to make their fortunes serving Jaroslav.

Standing astride the planks of the merchant ship he looked out to sea, shielding his eyes. The old, gnarled sailor watched him.

- *We shall arrive in Ladoga in the Autumn. The journey will be simple enough.*

Harald turned to him, and pulled up his hood to cover his face.

- *You have travelled it before, old man?*

- *I am a trader, not a soldier. This is a common-enough journey. From here we cross the Inland Sea and down the mighty rivers all the way to Miklagard.*

- *Then we are in safe hands, old man.*

The sailor held out both his hands and shook Harald's.

- *If Jaroslav is expecting us, we shall be safe enough. It is not often that we go knarr-full with weapons.*

HARALD HARDRADA - THE LAST VIKING

- *We are safe enough. The weapons are to be used to fight Jaroslav's enemies.*

-*War is never a good thing for us traders.*

-*War produces shortages; and shortages means you can put up your prices old man.*

- *But it comes with the risk that ports will be closed, harbours shut against us so that we have no way of trading. The route through to The Empire is often blocked by pirates, who rob us and sink our ships.*

Harald looked at the old man, and saw the lines that marked his age and wisdom.

- *Then perhaps it is time to stop trading and join us. We shall fight your corsairs and win your treasures back.*

- *I'm not a fighting man. I would miss the roll and toss of the sea. This ship, the Long Serpent, is the only home I have known. What good would I be with sword and shield?*

- *As much as I with sail and rope in hand.*

They both smiled and the sailor ran his hand along the edge of the ship, feeling its smooth contours.

- *This is my weapon, this boat. And this route is my home. You Norwegians have started to sail westward. There may be rich pickings there but the seas are wilder and life shorter.*

The sailor held out a hand:

- *I am Soren Sorenson, named for my father.*

As Harald stretched out his hand, the sailor added:

- *I know who you are. Your reputation runs before you. The hood and your silence cannot hide you, Harald Sigurdsson. You are the dead king's brother, and a brave man at that.*

The sailor watched him return to his place at the bow alongside the prow that rose up high above the ship's deck, the serpent's tongue stretching out over the sea. He smiled to himself. *This*

HARALD HARDRADA - THE LAST VIKING

young Prince thinks we are blind. Even in Sweden, his reputation runs before him. This is not a man content to serve others. Boy kings or Rus emperors beware.

The Long Serpent cut through the water. Some distance in front of them The Yearning sailed, and aboard it young Eilif. The sailor knew him better than he knew this Norwegian Prince. His father, the earl, was an honest man, and his son was made in his image. *They will come to blows these two captains.*

The days passed, and moons waxed and waned. By the time Ladoga could be seen with its wide-mouthed estuary and the fjord running inland, they were all pleased to be stepping ashore. Beards were longer and tempers shorter. On the journey the sailor noted how hard a task-master their captain was. But he was a fair man, asking no man to do what he himself could not. But beware the man, soldier or sailor who crossed him. One such, a young soldier, with a wispy beard and bright red hair, had mysteriously gone overboard the night after he'd argued with the captain. No-one knew for certain but it was assumed by all, that Harald had lightened the load by one. At the harbour entrance stood huge wooden piles, where chains hung loose, their rusty links sounding like bells in the autumn mist. As he had done often on this voyage, Harald went to Soren to seek an explanation.

- If Jaroslav didn't want us to enter the chains would be linked across the harbour and old hulks would block the entrance.

Harald shielded his eyes against the rising sun and saw the harbour walls, the open estuary and the wide river running away from them.

- But it is open to us, so we are obviously welcome. This is Ladoga.

HARALD HARDRADA - THE LAST VIKING

- Ladoga. And every time I arrive it grows bigger. When I first came, there was nothing here. Just an opening leading inward to the Great Inland Sea and we didn't stop except for a woman.

And he smiled at the memory of it.

- Now there are more women ready to open their legs than there are fish swimming in the harbour.

Harald had missed female company and was eager to see if such a claim was true.

- And what about you, old man. Will you stop for a woman, or sail on down river to Miklagard?

- I stay here, soldier. I work for Jaroslav now. Like you.

- Then perhaps we shall share a ship again, Sorenson.

And the old sailor nodded, touched his grey forelock and took his place among the ropes and sails, all the while watching Harald move down into the belly of the ship, where the men were mustering. The Long Serpent and The Yearning slipped into the harbour and Sorenson watched as his captain made sure their boat was tied up first. Standing in ranks alongside the wooden jetty stood the Varangian Guard. The sailor knew of them only by reputation: the seasoned battle-hardened Viking troops who were Jaroslav's personal bodyguard. He counted them; they stood five deep, in ten rows. Five hundred men, all of them armed with steel and plate. And he watched Harald as he jumped onto solid ground and stood a moment to regain his land-legs. After a few moments he was joined by the young earl. Sorenson moved across the boat so that he could hear them talk together.

- Quite a show, Harald. Is this our welcome to Rus?

- Look at them, Eilif, one day they shall be under my command. These are Viking men who need a true Viking leader.

HARALD HARDRADA - THE LAST VIKING

And the sailor's gaze moved to focus on the man who stood at their head, facing the two travellers. He sat astride a horse, flanked on either side by

- *Welcome, friends. I welcome you, Harald, as I welcomed your brother before you. Here in person. I hope you will stay longer than he did, and that your return is more successful. And you too Eilif, you are welcome, not just for your father' sake, but for your own. I have heard much of you and your bravery.*

It was Harald who spoke, moving towards him, cautiously as the flanking guards moved forward on their horses.

- *Thank you, Grand Duke. For my brother's sake as well as my own. I have heard your name from far away. And I believe it is with good reason you are called Jaroslav the Wise. I trust to your wisdom, and to your mercy.*

And the sailor watched as Harald knelt before him, and laid his sword on the ground. And the sailor understood that Harald was as wise as the Grand Duke. Eilif stepped forward then knelt so that he was alongside Harald. He lay down his shield.

- *Together, Grand Duke Jaroslav, we have come to serve you, in payment for your hospitality.*

The two men were signalled to rise and the soldiers and sailors on board the two ships climbed aboard. They were to stay in the harbour town for a few days before making their way to Novgorod, along the river trade route to the court of Jaroslav in the city.

The old sailor left the ship reluctantly, his sack thrown over his shoulder. He was much more comfortable on board. The harbour had few delights for him these days; expensive ale, watered weak; expensive women, talkative and tiring. No. The Long Serpent was a better place for him. He would sneak back much later, when it was dark and when the crew-master was in his cups or in a woman, and find a place to sleep in the belly of the ship. He watched as Harald and Eilif wandered through the town, following their progress, until they settled at an old tavern, its sign hanging above the doors: *The Black Bear.* There he left them. The doors swung shut behind Eilif and Harald. They were ready to make up for lost time.

The next two days were compensation enough for their cramped, cooped up journey as both the men sampled the delights of the harbour tavern. The women entertained them at night and the days were passed in eating and sleeping. Gradually they felt their strength returning and they emerged, their beards trimmed and in good humour. They were popular guests especially with the young women: generous with their money as well as their seed and the word spread about these two Viking warriors who were friends of The Grand Duke. But they were ready to move south. Jaroslav and his guards had gone ahead of them across the land. They would follow along the rivers and waterways that would take them to the heart of Jaroslav's empire. Back on board their ships they prepared for the journey. The old sailor was already aboard. He knew the drill. He had taken this journey so many times, following the river courses south. This was a journey his grandfathers had made, along the Dnieper, where so many Vikings had made and lost their fortunes. The Varangians as they were known here. It was Sorenson, that Harald sought out once they had set sail.

- *So, old man, did you get your fill in Ladoga?*

- *The town's delights are wasted on me, Sigurdsson. I slept aboard The Serpent.*

HARALD HARDRADA - THE LAST VIKING

- Alone, old man?

- With my ghosts. There are plenty enough of them. You must have ghosts too?

- I spare my thoughts for the living, Sorenson. The dead can look after themselves.

-Do they not haunt you, Harald, at night when you see them at your sword's end?

- I have no memory of them. They were enemies who died so that I could live.

And the sailor's wise smile returned.

- Then you are a lucky man, Harald Sigurdsson. For you can kill in clear conscience. You will be a great soldier.

- I am already a great soldier, Sorenson. As I'm sure you know.

And slowly, manoeuvring the river course, the boats sailed southward. It was winter, and sleet fell onto the boats when they finally arrived in Novgorod. Harald and Eilif were glad to leave the boats behind, and were welcomed into Jaroslav's court. Life was changing for both the Viking lords. They would lead men into battle soon enough but for the winter they would take shelter in the pleasant surroundings of a royal court.

Harald and Eilif were ready at last. They were established commanders of their own troops of Varangian Guards who were the duke's private army. These Vikings were proud to be led by men like themselves, and welcomed the leadership of two great noblemen. News from the Poles was everywhere. The rebellion was gaining strength and Jaroslav saw his power slipping away. The two Norwegians and their Varangian Guards were given the task of teaching the rebellious Poles a lesson. Their two ships were ready for the journey. Loaded again with arms they sailed down the river towards the battle, leaving the fortifications of Novgorod behind. There was little privacy on a longship, and Sorenson watched the Viking Prince as he stood, legs astride, imperiously commanding the crew and the soldiers. He saw the girl, too, smuggled aboard late at night, and she mingled with the others, the cooks, the sail-makers, the whores. But this woman was none of them. She had served in Jaroslav's court. Sorenson remembered her accompanying the Grand Duchess. *She* would not be shared amongst the men. She was his woman, chosen to serve his needs alone, almost certainly a gift from Jaroslav himself. She kept aloof, seeing herself as special. And at night he heard them together, talking after they had made love together. Always the same. She feared he would tire of her and then send her away to find solace with the other men. She spoke with a Rus accent, struggling with the language of her prince. He understood enough, even spoke a bit of this language. Two years among the Rus had not been wasted.

- *You will take me with you? Let me stay with you?*
- *Hush now. Come back to bed. We shall keep each other warm.*

They lived as man and wife. Sorenson knew the women on board would be shielded from the fighting, when it came, and they would build the new villages and towns, taken as plunder and help populate them.

- *I want to stay with you, my Prince. Become your Princess.*

Sorenson smiled to himself, as he stood, watching the ship's slow progress through the night crossing the mighty lake, like an inland sea. Harald Sigurdsson would not marry a Rus peasant, he was certain of that. His marriage would be an alliance, a weapon of war. This woman would be discarded as soon as she outlived her usefulness. Sorenson had seen enough of this prince to know he would tire of her whining. And once he did...

Spring sunshine warmed them in the daytime. And at last they came upon the mouth of the great river that flowed south and west. The river the Rus called Shelon. All along the banks were Polish soldiers, ready to fire arrows down onto their heads. Whatever doubts Sorenson had about the prince, he could not help but marvel at his courage and bravery. The two generals fought side by side, attacking the raiding parties and returning to dress their wounds, before sailing on and harrying more of the rebels. And each night he would return to the Rus girl and make love to her beneath the stars. They lived as man and wife, but the old sailor knew it could not last.

The end came quicker than he'd imagined. They were moving on again, along the river. The moon was shielded by thick heavy cloud. It had rained all day and more was threatened. Despite the warm summer nights, most of the men had wrapped themselves against the rain, their snores filling the air, vying with the biting insects that surrounded them. Sorenson was on watch. It was the girl's voice he heard first.

- *You promised me. I would be your Princess. You promised me.*

He saw Sigurdsson stand, and lift the bundle high above his head. It was heavy and awkward and sagged either side of his powerful arms. Then the splash. And the girl was gone, and with her went all her dreams of being a princess.

HARALD HARDRADA - THE LAST VIKING
REPUTATION

I watch him, this tall blond warrior, and I know what he wants from me. But I will not give it to him. He has taken my land, killed my brothers and now he wants a final betrayal. I know this man, by reputation. It had preceded him down-river, and it has us beaten before we start our fight. But we fight on. We will always fight on. This is our land, and the cursed High Duke with his Varangian hordes have come to steal it along with our gold and our women and children. But we will fight them. With every last breath we will fight them. There will be no vow of allegiance. He can never take that oath from me. And now it is almost over. I am bound; he has cut out my tongue and he has a final torture left for me. This is the man they call Hardrada in his own language. Ruthless. Savage. And it is an epithet well-earned for he spares no-one in this fight. My own wounds are testament to his savagery. And if I could speak I would tell him he is wasting his time. I am a Polish fighter. I cannot be cowed.

Jaroslav had ambitions which ran south and east. He wanted to expand the Rus Empire and control all the trade to its cities. The Varangian army were the perfect weapon to unleash on the Poles, who wanted to regain their homeland, occupied by the tyrant Grand Duke. The Varangians were mercenary soldiers, not interested in land. They would be happy paid in gold and whatever they could loot from the rebel armies they conquered in the Duke's name. And the two men who led them were certainly expertly remorseless. Eilif was a tall youth, strong of arm and loved by his men, loved for his father's name and reputation. Harald was feared by his men, and admired as a warrior; tall and strong and merciless. He was a leader who brooked no disobedience; he was acquiring a reputation the length of the Rus Empire. They had travelled southward and cleared much of the territories of rebel Slavs and Poles. Everywhere they went they left behind them death and destruction. Men were slaughtered, children drowned and women used and abused in nights of orgiastic drinking and rape. The Varangians were rightly feared, and none more than their two leaders, Eilif and Harald. And Jaroslav's hold on his conquests stayed strong. Harald had learned the art of leadership from his brother, but his ruthlessness was all his own work.

It was late Summer. The heat and the mosquitoes were both becoming intolerable, and there were mutterings from the men about returning home to the court at Kiev where even the barracks were preferable to this. Eilif and Harald held a council. Their two armies had finally met up. Most of the time, Eilif had harried from the north, chasing the rebels southward where Harald's men slaughtered them. It was Harald who had devised the tactics; not least because there was more glory, and more loot for his men with such an arrangement. After their council, they called together their boat crews and promised them that there would be one more battle this summer, and then they would return home, where the gold and treasures would be divided between them. They would return to Novgorod before the winter, and leave behind the mosquitoes that tormented them. There were cheers and extra rations were drunk. In the morning they sailed south again.

HARALD HARDRADA - THE LAST VIKING

The two men stood facing each other. One his arms at his side, his long blond hair hanging loose, his body broad and bloodied, though the blood was not his. The other was bound hand and foot, and the rope that bound him held him fast to a solitary tree. He was tall too, but he hung limp, his body wrecked, covered in blood which still ran from his mouth and his arms. They watched each other, across the clearing a hundred yards or so from the river where the Varangians drank to surfeit. It had been a bloody day but it was over. Or almost over.

- *It's a simple question, Pole.* Harald spoke in the man's own language. His ear was quick and he learnt from the captured women and children.

– *You must take the oath. And seeing as you cannot speak it now, you must write your name. You must acknowledge the right of your Emperor, The Grand Duke to all these lands. Just nod. Just give me a sign and you will be free to return with us. We shall mend your wounds, assuage your pain. Come, man, a nod is all I need from you. You are a brave soldier but your fight is over.*

You will have nothing from me. Nothing. The fight will be taken up by others. In time my son will pick up a sword. We shall never give up. But, of course, he cannot hear me.

It was the woman who spoke. She was sitting further off. Her hands and feet were bound too, and she had been left slumped on the edge of the clearing, to where she'd been dragged. To where the man, her man, could see her. Her body was hardly covered, and in this clearing, in the shadow of the trees it began to grow cool. He could see how the cold air affected her body: the gooseflesh on her thighs and shoulders, where the skin was exposed; the tightening of her breasts under the flimsy cloth that was draped from beast to thigh. In contrast he felt his own body grow hot. He wanted her, but he would wait. If the soldier gave him what he wanted, then perhaps he would take her anyway.

- You are wasting your breath, Viking. This man will never acknowledge Jaroslav. He is a despot, a tyrant, a man who hunts down and kills his fellow Slavs. This man will give his life first. You have seen it for yourself. When he will not speak the words, you cut out his tongue, but still he will not give you what you want.

Harald watched her as she spoke. Handfuls of her hair had been pulled out in her struggle, some of it lying in clumps near her.

- Do you think he can be won so easily? Do you think he could love me more than he loves our nation? More than our freedom?

But I do love her, this woman who has borne me one child and will bear me another soon. More than my life. He is looking at her now, and I know what is in his mind. I know he means to break me.

- I hope for your sake you are wrong. His eyes have been spared just for this. And Harald took his sword and moved towards her.

- Do your worst, Viking. Murder me if you must, but you shall have nothing from him except his hatred.

How brave she is, this woman. Braver than many of my fellow-soldiers who have cringed before him and begged his mercy. He gives none. But she doesn't flinch. He takes the sword and cuts the cloth from her body. He expects her to respond, to scream out perhaps. But this woman is not afraid. Not of death, nor of worse things that may come. He stands in front of her.

- If the signs are to be believed you are carrying his child, woman. Would it not be better for you all if he just gave me what I want?

- This child will never be born into this world. Jaroslav can have my body. He can have all of our bodies but he cannot take away our freedom.

HARALD HARDRADA - THE LAST VIKING

- It is not Jaroslav who will have your body... And he knelt down behind her, his sword at her breast.

How brave she is, this woman. How I would love to nod, to sign his paper. He has cut her breast. He watches me, waits for a sign. But there will be no sign. Now he stretches her out on the floor. Inside I scream Yes. Yes. Yes. But he will not have my name. He will not have my name.

As the ships sailed north again, Sorenson watched his captain. He sidled up to him.

- Does the irony of all this not occur to you, Sigurdsson?

There were very few men in the world who he would allow to call him Sigurdsson. And no others here on this journey.

- I have little time to spend thinking about irony, old man.

- You are here, fighting Jaroslav's War...

- The Grand Duke has Viking blood, from generations ago...

- ... But this war of his is against those who have been occupied. Is that not exactly what you fought against in Stikelstad? The occupation of Norway by a foreign King? But perhaps I speak too boldly.

He watched the prince turn it over in his mind. He saw the smile.

- You are right, old man. There was a long pause, and he was aware of the noise of the crew around him. *– You speak too boldly.* And he moved away, to stand beneath the high prow. The chests that had once been full of weapons were full now of gold and jewels. The men carried their swords hanging from their sides, or left them close by when they hoisted and lowered sails. He had heard the name that the men had given him: Hardrada. And he knew there was justification for such a title. Both the captains were ruthless, but this one, Harald Sigurdsson, it was he who was Jaroslav's arm. And he remembered the fate of all those who

stood against him, or those who merely displeased him. The story had come to him of the soldier and his wife and what he had done to them. Both left in a pitiable state in a clearing, he with no tongue, left to die from his wounds, and his wife, her body hacked to pieces and raped in front of the husband. But perhaps this had not happened. Perhaps this was no more than the myth that was Harald Sigurdsson, Prince of Norway. They had set off too late and now they must sail northwards again across freezing lakes, until they arrived at Kiev. Cold hands hoisted sails and rowed the ships. Hands and faces were raw with the biting winds and the snow blinded them. But the captain seemed impervious to it all. He stood tall and erect on board every day, keeping his own council. When they did make landfall, the two captains came together and drank long into the night, and in the morning they returned to their ships. Two leaders, shoulder to shoulder, hacking away at Poles and Slavs until there was nobody left to fight. Mercenaries leading their own army back to the court of their employer. It suited them all: the Varangians grew rich; the captains grew richer still. And Jaroslav kept control of his empire. And he, the sailor Sorenson, kept his mouth firmly shut. He was not one to rock the boat.

At Kiev the two Viking captains were welcomed with a feast. Kiev was a wonderful city and the palace was its jewel. With high majestic walls and tall pinnacle towers, it was more than just a fortress, it was a luxurious home, with ideas for its construction borrowed from all over the world. The Grand Duke himself welcomed them into the Dining Hall, where all the high-born sat, and the duke's own family - wife, sons and daughters – were the grandest of them all. It was Jaroslav himself who stood for the welcome cup.

HARALD HARDRADA - THE LAST VIKING

- Viking brothers, you are welcome. Since we last saw you, there has been much written and sung in your praises. Our kingdom is safer for your courage and bravery.

From her seat further down the table, Elisiv watched the fair-haired god. He was taller than any other man in the room, and more handsome too, despite the scar that ran along one side of his face, from ear to jaw. A scar from the battle at Stikelstad she had been told by her mother. She fell in love with him straight away, with this reincarnation of Harald the Fairhair, whose stories had filled her head since she was a toddler. And now he was here, in her father's palace. It was fate. Harald stood in response to his host's welcome, aware of all eyes upon him.

- His Majesty gives more praise than is due. We fought hard and we defeated his foes, and we do it willingly for the hospitality he shows us, and for the hospitality he has shown in the past to other Viking Kings and Princes.

And Elisiv trembled inside. She may only have been twelve but she knew, she just knew that this man, this fair-haired god, would be the man she would marry. Now she just had to convince her father of the value of such a match. She noticed how Jaroslav made a signal to one of the guards who stood at the closed door. He turned and left and returned almost immediately with a young boy. Elisiv saw at once the cloud that darkened Harald's face. The boy was taken to her father.

- We have welcomed you as we did your older brother, King Olaf, who now is sainted in your lands. And we have welcomed too his son, Magnus, a king in exile.

Elisiv watched Harald as he regained his composure.

- You have quite a collection of lost princes, Grand Duke.

And a laugh moved around the hall. Harald sat again and the boar was brought, still on the spit, dripping with juices, and carved pieces were set on the shiny metal platters. The Grand Duke held the meat in his hand, paused and looked at Harald.

- *Lost Princes rarely stay lost for long. When thrones are reclaimed, alliances can be built. Marriages can bind our families and our shared blood will rule in peace and harmony.*

The noise grew, and the court ate. Young Prince Magnus took his place next to Harald. As they ate, Elisiv managed to squeeze her way further up the table, taking Anastasia with her. Stasia was younger by three years, and the two sisters fought all the time, but Elisiv had to acknowledge that with her fair curls and fair skin she was good bait to trap a Prince. She was almost the same age as Young Magnus, and had already done a fair amount of flirting with him, as well as other of the "lost princes" who stayed in the court.

- *May I introduce my sister, Anastasia, Harald.*
- *Indeed, Elisiv. She is a welcome addition to our company.*
- *She and Magnus have been companions since he arrived here.*

Harald looked at her, and she saw the smile that began in his eyes and spread to his mouth.

- *And you, Elisiv? Who is your companion?*

Her heart fluttered. She was in the presence of a god and he deigned to talk with her.

- *I am much too old to need a companion, Prince Harald.*

And she watched as his eyes took her in, weighed her up. And she saw too, how his eyes strayed to the fairer face of Stasia. And she felt her face redden. It was no matter. Harald would be hers. She was determined.

Their plates and cups were never empty and soon the only light came from the torches that stood in sconces around the walls. And as always, speech turned to more serious matters. Despite their low, secretive tones, she heard Magnus and Harald speaking together. They discounted her; it was always the same. But she heard everything and understood much. It was Magnus who spoke first. He was an earnest, serious boy.

- *When will you return, uncle, to reclaim our lands in Norway? When will you hold high again the Golden Dragon banner of my dead father?*

- *When we are ready, Magnus. When the time is right. The Dragon will roar again.*

- *And then with God's help we shall throw Cnut off the throne.*

- *With God's help, little nephew? We shall need more than that. I believe that God rewards those who fight their own battles. If we are to wait for Divine Intervention...'*

'It must be through His help, Uncle Harald...'

'God fortunes the brave, Magnus. Are you brave?' And Elisiv heard the tremor in the young boy's voice.

- *With His help, I shall be brave, Uncle.*

- *But alone, you and I will not move the fat arse of Cnut.* Magnus blushed at the word, but Elisiv laughed to herself. How different were these two princes!

- *We shall need soldiers and we shall need to arm them. And that will take a lot of money, a lot of gold. Then when I am ready...*

- *We shall reclaim our kingdom.* Magnus smiled his small wispy smile. He turned away and missed Harald's final comment.

- *Reclaim MY kingdom!*

But Elisiv had heard it, and knew what was meant.

- *And now I shall take my leave of you. My bed calls and I am ready for it.* Elisiv watched him go. She saw him walk the length of the hall. At the door he glanced back. To her? No. It was Anastasia that had that last look.

- I beg, Grand Duke, to leave Rus, and journey south to Miklagard.
The old sailor's words had rolled about in his head. Jaroslav would
not stop until all the Slavic nations were united in a single empire,
ruled and controlled by the Grand Duke, and then what use would
Jaroslav the Wise have for him?
- What will you do in that great city? Jaroslav smiled at him. He
knew the answer all too well. *– Make your fortune, perhaps?*

Harald and Jaroslav stood in the shadow of the newly-built Golden
Gate. The Rus leader was proud of this visible sign of his power
and wealth.
*- This gate is a copy of the Golden Gate of Miklagard. Is this not
proof enough that this city of ours is as great as that city? Is it not
proof enough that our empire is as mighty? And when I have
finished the Great Church of Saint Sophia, then Kiev shall be as
glorious as that city. What can Miklagard offer that this wise duke
would need?*
- When I return it will be with riches for us both.
Harald watched him carefully, weighing him carefully.
- Am I not rich enough, Prince of Norway?
*- A mighty ruler can never have too much. A mighty ruler needs to
support an army, to conquer territory, to buy and sell Governors
and Earls... If you are to rival Miklagard, you must have its wealth.*
- If you are set on this, Harald, then you shall go with my blessing...
That was the easy part. If Harald was to be successful, he needed
an army to go with him. The 'Wise' ruler watched him below
hooded eyes. He waited...
- To be successful – for both of us – I need an army.

HARALD HARDRADA - THE LAST VIKING

- *I can let you have a small company of men. I will need to keep most of the Viking warriors. They are my personal bodyguard, and in Miklagard they will be too far from me. Eilif can stay here. He will lead them.*

- *And I shall return, galleys laden with gold, jewels, spices. You will be rich.*

The eyes never wavered, never left Harald's face.

- *As shall you, Harald. And how will I be certain you will return home this way, Prince?*

- *You have my word, Grand Duke. As a fellow Viking; by the blood of our ancient kin...*

Jaroslav's smile grew wide.

- *And if there are temptations on the way home that allow our ancient kin's blood to be forgotten?*

- *I shall send home all my treasures for safe-keeping. This is my surety, if my word is not enough.*

- *Your word is enough, Harald. But the treasure doubles the bond. There are vaults in Novgorod that lie empty. Fill them as you can. Prepare the boats you need. I grant you your wish. You can handpick the men you want to accompany you.*

Harald commissioned five ships, crewed by the four hundred men he chose, men who he knew to the bravest and best. Men who would follow him to Valhalla if he asked them. And their journey to Miklagard would be more than a treasure hunt, for those who had taken the Christian religion – as he had – it would serve as pilgrimage too, seat of the Holy Roman Emperor. Riches of pocket, and riches of soul. What more could they ask? And they would follow him. He bade farewell to Eilif and they spent their last night together drinking, and recounting their Rus adventures.

The ships were assembled at the dockside. Spring had arrived and the waters ran freely. Trees showed their early signs of renewal, and the farms that were scattered around Kiev showed evidence of the sown seed, the green shoots of the rye and barley crop had forced their way through the dark brown soil. He chose Sorenson to accompany him on board his own ship. He had formed a bond with the old sailor. There were few men with whom he could share his thoughts; few who would give tell him what they thought. Besides, he was a good sailor and there would be need of good sailors. The journey to Miklagard would be long and dangerous. Good sailors would be invaluable.

Iron-shielded vessels
Hugging close to shore,
Southward through the rainstorms
Through showers bleak and raw.
Sails adorned with colour
Approach now, Prince so bold.
Gleaming copper roofs and spires...
Byzantium Behold!

HARALD HARDRADA - THE LAST VIKING

MIKLAGARD

Sorenson had heard about the copper roofs; of course he had. Hadn't stories of them spread everywhere? He'd heard about the wide streets, the market places full of stalls selling exotic wares, the taste and purpose of which, an old sailor could only guess. He had heard about the silk route and the spice route, and of the money the captains made from those journeys, so long as they could escape the clutches of pirate marauders who hid in secret coves around the warm Mediterranean Sea. Yes, he'd heard about them, but to be here, to see them for himself... Sigurdsson had disappeared early on, after their first sunrise. And was nowhere to be seen. The old sailor knew enough about his captain to suspect he was busy jockeying his position, gaining access to the rich and powerful.

If you rub up against the wealthy the gold brushes into your pockets, his father had always said. Like him, his father had been a sailor, and had known how to read advantage. Now, Sorenson had his eyes, his ears and his pockets open, for whatever he could catch in this city of half a million souls, where farmers, traders, slaves and lords rubbed shoulders together. Yes, he had heard much, but nothing had prepared him for the sights and sounds. Kiev had been grand; but Miklagard – or Constantinople as he was going to have to get used to calling this city, in their strange tongue - was a whole new world, the centre of the Christian Empire. The city spread itself down to the sea, with the grand port-side buildings where merchants traded with the riches borne across the seas. Further in, a short walk away from the docks, through narrow passages and wide-open market squares, there stood the centre of this city. Here there were buildings dedicated to the display of art and sculpture. This was all new to Sorenson, who had never visited such a place before. Marble statues and paintings dazzled him, with rich coloured images of scenes from stories he knew well enough but had never seen portrayed so vividly. The Imperial Palace and the Circus were jewels in the crown, but the copper dome of the huge Cathedral was like the crown itself, and in the warm sunshine it shone like gold. He was satisfied to stand outside and watch. He hadn't embraced the new religion, as had the Princes and Kings of Norway; he preferred the old gods, who kept the ships upright, and the seas tamed. The sailor's gods. No, he was content to stand outside and marvel at its splendour, to take in its beauty. What happened inside was none of his affair.

The city also had strong walls, but its population still feared the world beyond; feared the Arab with his cruel heathen ways. So many of these men and women were themselves immigrants, refugees fleeing from the barbarism of the scimitar-wielders who sat outside and waited for their chance. Yes. This was a city for an ambitious captain, and if he, Sorenson could make his fortune marching with him, then he'd follow the Viking Prince.

Sorenson could see that Zoe liked what she saw. A Varangian army stood in ranks before her, and before them, this Northern Prince, whose reputation had flown before him, knelt in supplication. From his place in the ranks, Sorenson watched her face. She was already falling under his spell, despite her so-recent wedding to Michael, a convenience to secure her place as empress. Michael was, apparently, no great lover, but this blond Varangian looked as if he might be. This woman who had already buried one emperor, who'd died at his wife's hand so the rumours said, might have no qualms in finding another.

As well as an empress, Zoe was a woman of great beauty, regal, and in every way meeting the expectation of her reputation. Sorenson was no expert in women; his experience of them limited to a nagging, but loving wife, to whom he would return at the end of his journeys. He was too old to spend time in dalliance and lust. So he was no expert, but even to his untrained eye he saw a woman who bore her age with grace and elegance. She was every inch an empress, but every inch a woman too, and like all women she was susceptible to the charm of the Norse Prince, especially when he came with a Varangian army, reputed to be the greatest fighters in the world. Harald had come and conquered. Sorenson saw all this and smiled. Sigurdsson had called the guard together. All his negotiating in secret meetings had borne fruit, and now they stood in ranks; an army to be displayed before an Empress.

At her side sat Michael Catalactus, but it was clear to all that it was Zoe that wielded the power. But these were turbulent times: Bulgars, Arabs, and self-serving pirates all wanted to take what was hers, and she needed an army to protect her. Sorenson watched as Harald knelt before her; watched as she raised him up and her eyes never left him as she walked with him through the ranks. Harald knew his men well, and he had stories to tell of many of them, and she laughed as he recounted the foolishness of one, the bravery of another.

Somewhat removed from all of this stood another man. He was less impressed with this Viking Prince. Less impressed with the stories of his courage and ferocity. He was Georgios Maniakes. Standing at least as tall as Harald, Georgios was reputed to be a cousin of the empress; but he had ambitions to be greater than that. Or so Sorenson had heard. He looked to take Michael's place, and he saw the chemistry flowing between this fair-haired stranger and his empress. She beckoned to him and he bowed his head, making his way to where she stood, her arm linked with Prince Harald Sigurdsson. The two men looked at each other, and Sorenson smelt the tension, even from such a distance; smelt the odour given off by the rutting stag in his native woods, as he fought to control his herd. There would be trouble between these two men. Zoe took Georgios's hand in hers, and held both their hands. She turned first to Harald. She spoke to him in his native Norwegian, slowly because her accent was strong.

- *Georgios is my general. Such a brave man, and a handsome one.* And to Georgios she said:

- *This is Araltes. See how he comes to the aid of a poor woman. Georgios, I am certain we can make use of a man with such talents as he has. And such beauty.* She felt the tall general stiffen, bristling. She knew what games she was playing.

- *And such an army,* he replied. Then she dropped his arm and dismissed them both. They stood for a moment facing each other, before Georgios added:

- *Dismiss your men, Harald. It is too hot for them to stand in the noon sun, fully armed.* And Georgios Maniakes turned on his heel. But Harald did not dismiss his men. We stood for another hour until the shadows slanted away to the east. Only then did the men get the order to stand down. He had made his point. He called Sorenson to him, in his officer's quarters.

- *What do you know of this man, Sorenson? This Maniakes?*

- *He comes from Anatoli, Sigurdsson.* He saw the eyebrows arch...

– *A town on the island of Kriti, to the south.*

- *A Greek then.*

-*A Kritan certainly. It is said that he is closer to the Empress than a soldier should be.*

HARALD HARDRADA - THE LAST VIKING

- A cousin, I'd heard, Captain. As of this moment, I am a General, Sorenson. Equal in rank to this Greek. Be sure to use my title.

- Yes General. I shall be sure. As for this Maniakes, he is not a cousin, that is a story he likes to be told. No, he is a suitor, who has designs on the Empire. And Sorenson left him to think. It was not just Empress Zoe who could play games.

Harald waited for the summons to come, as he knew it would. He took two of his newly-promoted captains with him to the palace, as well as Sorenson,

- For you read men well, old man. And I need someone I can trust. Sorenson looked about him. The beauty of the outside was nothing compared to the opulence, the grandeur, that greeted them in the Great Hall of the Palace. The Empress was standing, tall, regal, with purple gown and golden shawl.

- Araltes, my General. I want you to take your army southwards. Sail to the islands and show the rebels that Empress Zoe is to be feared. Let them know the power of the Empire.

- Will we sail alone, Empress?

- Georgios will accompany you with his troop of men. He is my General, Araltes. He shall be yours too.

- My men only serve me, your Highness.

- They can serve you, Araltes, but you will serve Georgios. Sorenson watched the struggle inside the Viking General.

- You will be well rewarded for such loyalty.

At last he bowed, and Sorenson saw the smile pass between them. The lines were drawn, the game would play out.

Sorenson slipped the messenger into the camp, gave him food and water and let him sleep. He had been travelling for many months, and his message would wait no longer. He sent word to the general. The next morning, he brought him before Harald.

- *So kinsman. What words do you bring from my home?*

- *Your nephew has returned to take up the throne, my lord prince.*

- *And what of Cnut? Where is the tyrant now?*

- *Dead, my lord prince. And his son Harthacnut takes his place on the throne. But the Norwegian throne returns to its rightful owner. To Magnus, our sainted Olaf's son.*

- *And did this boy – this bastard boy – win back the throne by force of arms?*

- *By a shake of hands, my lord prince. The old Danish King had never managed to win the hearts and swords of the brave Norwegians.* The messenger looked directly at Harald for the first time.

– *The chieftains themselves carried him, shoulder high, and placed him on the high throne. He has their support. All of them. Your mother, Queen Ásta herself once sat beside him.* Harald dismissed him, gave orders that he be given money for his journey and to return to him again the next day before his long journey home. And to his departing back he said:

- *So this eleven-year-old boy has my throne.*

- *And what will my lord prince do now?* It was Sorenson who spoke. He was waiting by the door, where he had stood throughout.

– *Are we to return home?*

-*Would you like that old man?*

-*This is a fine city, Sigurdsson, but it is not my home. Nor yours.*

- *But there is still much to be done, battles to be fought, cities to be ransacked, treasures to be taken. And there is much to be thought on too.*

- *Indeed, General. There is much for you to do.*

HARALD HARDRADA - THE LAST VIKING

- And this boy will wait.

Harald dismissed his captain and stood in silence, giving time for the news to settle, for the nausea in his throat to subside. He saw the light dim, as a shadow appeared at the open doorway. It was Giorgio Maniakes, the General's General who stood in front of him.

- It is time, Araltes. Time to show what you can do.

Autumn in the Mediterranean was kinder than the hot summers. And for men armed and dressed for battle, the difference was noticeable. The warm breezes brought with them a restlessness, and they were only too keen to follow their generals into battle. During the hot summer months, they grew indolent, and kept out of the sun, drinking the wine until they fell asleep. Harald kept an eye on them. He wanted them ready, but he wanted them loyal. The days were shorter by the time they set sail. The galleys were set to patrol the seas around the Greek islands, places known well to Maniakes. The corsairs fled before them, no match for this armada. And as they sailed, and harried, and fought and slayed, Harald reminded his men who was their general. They were well-rewarded for their loyalty. Tribute was exacted in the name of the Empress, and it was a huge bounty, enough that some could be shared by Generals and warriors according to their needs. And Georgios and Harald grew rich, and their battle-hardened troops grew rich too. This was the true Viking tradition, exacting Danegeld on the islanders in return for a promise to keep them safe from the Arab dhows. These boats were fast and much more manoeuvrable, but they were outnumbered. However cruel this Varangian army seemed, at least they were Christian men. The

Arab were heathens, and were barbaric. From island to island they sailed, and the men were allowed enough young women to satisfy their growing lusts. And all the time, Harald kept watch on the chief enemy – Georgios Maniakes.

They had marched overland for several hours, pursuing the straggling islanders, who harried them all the way. Night fell earlier now, and Georgios gave the order to set up camp. The Varangians were the first to arrive, and they chose the higher ground for their tents, above the boggy ground. Once the men were settled, Georgios arrived. Sorenson knew what would follow.

- *Araltes, you must leave this camp here, and pitch tents further down. This place is reserved for my army.*

- *We arrived first, General, so we have taken our place first. If you had arrived first at our night quarters...*

- *Pitch yourselves lower down, Araltes. I command it.*

- *My men are not yours to command, General Maniakes. I am their leader. They take orders only from me.*

Georgios Maniakes rose to his full height, towering over even the Viking Prince.

- *I expect to be obeyed.*

- *Then you will be disappointed, General Maniakes. They follow my orders.*

- *And the Empress has made it clear to you that you follow my orders. And you will know that Empress Zoe and I are kin.*

Sorenson felt the air crackle, could almost see the lightning that flew between them. Would Sigurdsson tell him what everyone suspected, that his claim of kinship to the Empress was false. Both men stood for a seeming age. It was Sigurdsson who moved first.

- *In our country, Maniakes, it is a sin for kin to lie together...*

The knuckles of their hands were white as they gripped their swords, already drawn. Someone had to stop them, and Sorenson, emboldened by his fear of the alternative, stepped between them.

- *Our swords are best used to fight a common enemy, Generals. It is a simple matter to leave it to God to decide.* Maniakes turned his eyes to the old sailor, but his sword was held upward at hip-height.

- *Explain yourself, Captain Sorenson.*

- *You should draw lots, General, both of you and let fortune prevail. Once and for all.*

The dark-haired giant smiled, as though he had some plan hatching.

- *God will surely favour the Empress's man. Let's do as he says, Araltes.*

Harald waited a moment, looking at the smile on Maniakes's face. He took a step forward.

- *And how will I know that you will not cheat? Marking your own lots. To give God a helping hand?*

It was Sorenson who replied.

- *Both mark your lots but let a man with a blindfold draw them out.*

Both men were nervous now. One would have to give way. Maniakes knelt down, took two twigs from the ground and passed one to Harald. Both scratched initials on one and handed them to Sorenson, who took a leather-thonged purse from his pocket and placed them inside.

- *We shall bind your eyes, Captain Sorenson. You can draw them. You can do God's work.*

HARALD HARDRADA - THE LAST VIKING

Harald watched as he saw the blindfolded Sorenson's hand pull one from the purse. He snatched it and hurled it into the river that bubbled at their feet. The three men watched it disappear. Harald looked triumphant.

- *The owner of this lot shall take precedence, when riding, when rowing, when putting in at harbour, and when choosing ground for their tents. That was my lot. So all these shall be my rights.*

Georgios Maniakes's face was murderous. Sorenson feared that he would slay both of them.

- *And how are we to know that it was your lot you threw into the river? You have cheated me, Harald Sigurdsson. Why did you not let me see it?*

Harald put his hand on Maniakes's sword hilt and held it there while he spoke.

- *I speak true, Georgios. For proof, you need only look in the purse to see whose lot remains.*

It was some time later that Sorenson came across to meet his General as he stood watching the tents being pitched below them on the soggy ground.

- *You took a chance there, Sigurdsson. What made you so sure?*

- *I am a godly man, Sorenson, but I have learned not to trust God with such heavy decisions. So I gave the Lord a little help.*

Sorenson watched him as he looked down at the growing camp below. Then he smiled.

- *You scratched your lot with his mark.* God, it seemed, truly is wise above all things.

The next day, as so often happened, Georgios's troops were first into battle, so it was his troops that suffered the greatest losses. The giant General fought like a wild man, hacking at the fleeing Greek islanders, marching over their bodies where they fell. The Varangians were swift to follow, and to share the spoils. And so it was for the two months they marched together, and when they sailed into the Great Harbour at Constantinople it was with bulging chests of treasures, none bigger than that of the Varangian General. Trusted messengers took the hoard back to the treasuries of Jaroslav, where it was building into a vast fortune. It was this fortune that drove him on. It was this fortune that would see him fulfil his destiny.

- *Soon, I shall be ready.*

The Byzantine Army had returned. And the people greeted them all with cheers. Emperor Michael and his wife Zoe watched them parade with the tall giant general, Georgios Maniakes. And they were adored. But none was more loved than Araltes, the blond Warrior Prince, who had not returned to the city. Zoe feared most that in her charge, the Empire would lose its precious jewel. Jerusalem must not be allowed to fall to the Arab hordes. It was Araltes she trusted to keep this jewel safe.

HARALD HARDRADA - THE LAST VIKING

TALES

Brenn had something special to say to her son. It would not wait. She had spoken to old man Becken, who was fed up with his daughter Svana forever hanging around the forge making calf-eyed at her son. Svana was a beautiful girl. Graceful like the elegant white bird she was named for. Not like the raven that gave its name to Brenn! She would see him today.

Dag had been on the farm in Ringerike. Life had returned to much the same as he'd remembered as a boy, but he was no longer a boy. He had seen action; had been at Stikelstad with Olaf, who had become, since his death, so much more than a king. It was almost four years since he'd left his boyhood friend and companion-at-arms, and she knew he'd made it his business to find out as much as he could about the prince. He found clever cartographers who drew him maps and showed him where the Viking army had been. He had followed the prince with his finger, while in his heart Brenn knew he wished only to be alongside him in Kiev, and then along the rivers fighting rebellious Poles. Dag had difficulty understanding why Slavs were killing each other, until she had reminded him that Vikings had killed each other for years in his own lands: Danes and Norwegians set against each other. There had even been talk about Olaf having been murdered by his own soldiers. Together they had joined the dead king's mother on the journey to Nidaros, northwards along the great river Nid, the body purified, preserved and wrapped. There the doddery Bishop Grimkell led the service and his remains were laid to rest. Since then she had seen pilgrims moving up and down the country. But her son had stayed with here, working on the farm at Ringerike.

HARALD HARDRADA - THE LAST VIKING

It was for his mother's sake he had returned, and it was for her he remained. Dag wasn't a natural farmer. He preferred wielding a sword to pulling a ploughshare, but when Asgar, the smith who lived at the forge, died in a fall which burnt him to death, Brenn encouraged her son to take his place. He was strong and he could hammer metal into fine shapes to make the farm-tools that were needed. He was happier doing that, but she knew that each hammer blow that rang out reminded him of the clash of swords at Stikelstad. And any spare time he had was used to fashion swords and shields, for the day he would take up the fight again alongside Harald. When he returned. And she feared that day. He had lived at Ringerike forever. Only the battle had taken him away. That view of other worlds, of other roles had made him discontent. But each day he returned to the forge and struck hammer blows. And every day, Brenn would stand at the door of the forge, out of reach of the heat, her hands on her hips and smile to see him, leaving a cloth-wrapped lunch.

Messengers came and went, bearing news of Harald, and he ran his fingers along the maps seeking out the names of places beyond Kiev, where he knew his boyhood friend and prince, 'the boy', had become feared and admired. And he traced the routes the Viking sailors took deep into the empire of the Polish king. Slavs killing Slavs. All for land. And here he was on his own small patch, warm in the winter and baking in the summer. Safe where she could see him.

The news of Magnus was well-received. She had stayed in the manor house that sat at the centre of Ringerike, close to the dead Queen's other sons, who had built up large estates now, and who owned the farm that Brenn and she worked. But when the news broke that Cnut was dead and that Norway was to be returned to

HARALD HARDRADA - THE LAST VIKING

Olaf's line, there had been two whole days of celebration. And for the first time in her memory the country was no longer at war.

It was noon. She made her way down to the forge. Dag stopped his hammering. The ploughshare blades were sharp; he could testify to that. His finger had tested its blades and she could see where they had drawn blood. He stepped into the warm sunshine, which still felt cool after the heat of the furnace. He saw her approaching from the kitchen of the farmhouse where she worked for the old queen's daughter, Ingrid, and her husband the young earl. Brenn was in her mid-forties now, but she was as robust as ever.

- *I have brought food, Dag. Can we sit together and eat?*

- *I have much to do.* It was a game they played every day. She would come to the forge; she would ask the same question; he would always say he was too busy; but they would always eat together.

— *But I can spare a few minutes.*

Brenn sat close to him. She smelt the warm sweat of him, his smell as familiar as her own.

- *It's not just food I bring...* and she unwrapped the small parcel and handed him the rye bread. And the game continued:

- *Eel again, mother?*

- *I know it's your favourite...* And the smiled as he pulled with his teeth at the fresh fish. He turned and looked at her:

— *And what else have you brought your hard-working son?*

- *News, Dag. Good news.*

- *Well let's have it then. If it tastes as good as the eel, it will slip down well.*

- *Svana has asked to speak with you.*

- *Svana?*

- *The Becken girl. She speaks of you all the time.*

95

HARALD HARDRADA - THE LAST VIKING

Brenn watched her son redden.

– She probably says too much, mother.

- She speaks the truth. She and you are often together.

- She works alongside you in the kitchen, mother. What should I do? Ignore her?

- The old man has given his blessing?

- To what?

She knew he was not playing. He really didn't know!

- She wants to marry you. She says she can't wait until you get round to asking her father...

Brenn enjoyed seeing her son blush.

- ... Nor can she wait until the baby appears...

- The baby?

Dag's face was completely red now, hotter than the fire he tended.

Tjodolv Arnorsson liked nothing better than to watch the sheep in the fields. From this position he could see them, grazing peacefully in the meadows above the farms. He could tell from the way she made her way up the hill that Brenn was coming to him, and that would mean trouble. Brenn would want something from him. A verse no doubt about something or other. But he had more important work to do. And while it was still in his memory he wanted to push on with it. He did not want to be disturbed. Brenn knew this as she approached. She liked the boy. They were all boys to her. Tjod, as she always called him, had grown up with her boy. He was like one of her own, like Harald. But he had very different skills. Tjod was neither fighter nor farmer. He wasn't actually a very good shepherd, but what skills he had were unique in Ringerike. Young Arnorsson, like his father before him was a skald, who could weave stories into magic; who could command language to obey his moods and bring to life the news he heard. He could make the everyday into an epic adventure. She was close enough now to see him scratching at the wooden block, carving the latest news, rune by rune. She stopped to catch her breath. The hill was steep. She called him.

- *Tjod!* The boy was being deliberately deaf. – *Tjod!*

He placed the woodblock and the chisel down beside him and gave an exaggerated sigh.

- *What is it Brenn? Can't you see I'm busy? If you disturb me now then the ideas will have floated out of my head, settle on the ground and be munched with the grass by my sheep.*

- *That's what I want, Tjod. Your words. There is a wedding planned and only you can do justice to it.*

- *Which wedding do you mean? Is the boy king taking a bride? Perhaps you speak of Prince Harald far away in Byzantium? Or is it The Boy King himself who has found a wife.*

- *Now then, Tjodolv Arnorsson, there's no need to play games. You know perfectly which wedding I'm talking about.*

- *Dag and Svana! The peasants of Ringerike. Why should I waste my talents on such as those?* And he picked up his work again. - *I am busy rendering the adventures of Prince Harald in Miklagard. What could be more important than that?*

Brenn knew how to get his attention.

- *I can pay. I wouldn't expect such an excellent wordsmith as you to do it for nothing.* Flattery and money always worked. He put his work down, looked over the sheep and then asked:

- *How much?*

HARALD HARDRADA - THE LAST VIKING

The wedding day itself was everything Brenn had hoped it would be. That was no accident. It certainly wasn't any thanks to Dag. He seemed content to marry the girl in a small back room. But she would have none of it. Ingrid was only too pleased to grant everybody the day off, if she could arrange for it to coincide with the Harvest Gathering Festival. Brenn agreed, and Dag and Svana would be wed before the baby was born. The harvest that year was a good one. The summer had been long and dry, and the fruit was swollen and ripe. There were rye cakes and fresh fish; boar had been slaughtered, and Brenn herself had supervised the boy on spit-turning duty. At sunset, all the villagers made their way home much the worse for wear after taking far too much of the apple wine and honey mead. She was ready for her own bed, once her son and his new wife had departed for theirs. The last man left was Tjod.

- *Thank you. The verse was beautiful, as I knew it would be, and we shall keep the woodcut forever. You are a fine skald, young Arnorsson.*

- *And you are an excellent judge of good verse, Brenn.*

The skald made his way home. The wedding verse had been simple enough. He had spoken with the parents and found out some special things about the bride and groom; special things that had been cut into the woodblock and hung above the anvil where Dag worked. Tomorrow he had to finish the work he had started. News had come from Harald. He had left Miklagard and journeyed to Jerusalem. He had fought battles in the lands of the Saracens. Victorious and booty-laden he had moved on to Sicily. He had heard the tales and started writing them out:

HARALD HARDRADA - THE LAST VIKING

The young gold-hunter strove,
Bravely risking life and limb;
In the Land of the Saracen
Eighty cities fell to him.
Then on the plains of Sicily
This warrior waged his war
Forcing lands to submit
Neath the fire-mountain's roar.

Brenn brought the news to Dag. The baby was sucking at Svana's breast. But she knew he would want to know.

- *Sit down, mother. Eat with us. Svana has prepared a meal and we have enough to share.*

- *There is a new messenger in town. He comes from Harald himself. I have it even before Tjod can finish it.*

- *He will make a better job of it than you. Come sit.*

And Brenn told them what he had heard and even the baby kept still and quiet while she relayed the stories that had travelled half a continent. She told stories that made her proud that she had brought up this boy prince.

- *They tell of fierce battles in strong fortified towns in Sicily, which is an island that sits beneath a volcano. Harald is a master-strategist* to hear the tales. Dag smiled. He knew for himself the truth of it. Even with the anticipated exaggeration, the stories would have more than a grain of truth.

- *He used birds to set fire to the first, using their homing instincts to carry fiery reeds back to their nests under the eaves in the town. It seems the townsfolk surrendered and he granted mercy for all those who begged for it.*

HARALD HARDRADA - THE LAST VIKING

- Harald can charm the birds to do his work for him. I just wish I had been beside him to see it for myself.

Svana laid the babe aside.

- And I am glad that you are not.

And Brenn knew she had kept her son safe.

- There was a second town, another siege, where the citizens were heavily armed and could see the army camped outside its walls. This time, he dug tunnels where a stream flowed through a ravine, which was hidden from the sentries. Finally, they broke through the floor surprising them all. Harald's Viking guard killed most of them where they sat, still drinking. They opened the gates and the Viking army streamed into the town. Those who begged for mercy lived.

She could see that as much as he enjoyed hearing about his friend's adventures, he regretted that he was not with him, alongside him.

- And there is a third tale too, of how he feigned death so that they would open the gates to give him a splendid funeral. When the guards had finished it was the town's people that were dead, and Harald and the soldiers were fortunes richer.

They toasted 'the boy's' success and finally Brenn had to be helped home. When Dag returned his wife and baby were asleep by the fire.

1066

HARALD HARDRADA - THE LAST VIKING

WE LIE AT ANCHOR ON THE RIVER OUSE and plot our strategy to meet the English army led by the Earls Morcar and Waltheof. Harald organises his forces so that it separates into two groups: one follows the river, the other he leads inland towards the great dyke, with the Landwaster banner flying in the wind. Suddenly they are upon us, seemingly victorious, as we flee along the dyke. The English soldiers follow us, just as he had planned. Then Harald sounds the attack and we turn and fight against the Saxon army. Ahead of us, Harald, tall with arms swinging this way and that, cuts a swathe through them. The dyke fills up with fallen men, and the dyke's water flows red. The English army takes flight, some up-river, some down, chaotic, disorganised, and Harald shouts at their backs: 'Stay! Fight!' In the end the bodies lie so thick on the swampy ground that our army crosses the boggy land without getting our feet wet.

> **Men were lost in the muddy dyke,**
> **Viking and English men.**
> **Warriors perished where they fell,**
> **Food for carrion.**
> **Young Prince Olaf brave and true**
> **Followed those who fled,**
> **Running ahead of his father,**
> **To avenge the Viking dead.**

1039 - 1047

All men knew
Brave Harald fought.
Savage battles,
Dearly bought.
With bloody steps
Destroying peace.
Eagles feed;
Wolves feast.

HARALD HARDRADA - THE LAST VIKING
FIRE

- It defies logic. It cannot be.

Sorenson was on board Prince Harald's ship. They had taken shelter from the storm, in a make-shift harbour on a tiny island. In the distance they could see the Turkish fleet, pirates and marauders, also moored up, on another island, blocking his escape when the winds changed. They outnumbered the Varangian fleet ten to one.

- If we have a weapon, Sorenson, then we must use it on our enemies before they use it on us.

The five ships had been at sea almost a month now. They were on their way back to Miklagard, from where rumours of a revolution had reached them. Harald was sworn to defend the empress and the Varangian guards were needed. The storm had held them up. Sorenson was in a foul mood. Like all sailors, he was happiest when the sail was spread and the wind carried them onward. Taking shelter was not his idea of being a sailor. In the years he had served this Viking Prince, he had seen his fortune grow, but at a cost to his mortal soul. His General was a ruthless man, laying waste the towns that opposed him, and showing no mercy to those who surrendered. And now this.

Harald was in a hurry. The ships that blockaded him were waiting for him to make a run for it. They would never be able to outrun them; the five ships were fully laden, and were larger and slower through the water. There was nothing else for it. Harald was adamant.

- Sea Fire is our only answer.

- It is against nature Sigurdsson. The two words do not go together.

HARALD HARDRADA - THE LAST VIKING

- But I have seen it, Captain. With my own eyes.

- And I have heard the rumours, General, but that is all they are. "Greek Fire" I have heard it called. And even if it were true, to bring this magical fire on board a ship is courting disaster.

- And what alternatives do we have, Sorenson?

- We must send for reinforcements. Maniakes' s fleet is two days away. Together we shall defeat this motley armada.

- And give that pumped-up Gyrgir the satisfaction of saving us? No Captain. We must do this ourselves and we shall be the heroes of tales down the ages.

Sorenson knew that Harald was seeking immortality. From the very beginning he had skalds on board the ships who carved his adventures on skins and bark, to be taken back as to Norway as reports of his success. The stories would enlarge his reputation so when the time came to fight Magnus for the throne... Harald interrupted him.

- Bring me the Byzantine sailors. They will have knowledge of the recipe for this weapon.

- I tell you Sigurdsson, I cannot be captain of a vessel which has this fire on board.

- Bring me the sailors, and with them Ulf Ospaksson and Halldor the Icelander. They were with me at Stikelstad, and have been loyal throughout our adventures.

- I am loyal, Prince Harald, but what you ask me is...

- Go, Sorenson. Take your place on the second ship. Be its captain. We shall use the fire to clear a path for you to escape.

Sorenson recognised the General's mood. He was not to be shaken. He was called obdurate by his friends; and stubborn by others. He would not be shaken. But neither would he, Sorenson. He had seen too many fires at sea to know that little good comes of mixing the elements which are sworn enemies.

HARALD HARDRADA - THE LAST VIKING

In the flashing light of the storm, Sorenson collected his sack, checked that the long knife which was his trusted weapon was tucked into his belt, and made his way to the sheltered side of the ship, where the crew sat waiting for the storm to pass. He spoke briefly with the two Byzantine sailors who sat together, speaking their own language. Captain Sorenson spoke with them, in their own tongue, pointed towards the prow of the ship, where the General still stood, ignoring the wind and rain. They liked their Varangian Captain, but were more fearful of their scarred General. They had been useful during the voyages; they knew the islands well, and their knowledge of the tides and currents was precious. It had been that knowledge that, until now, had kept them ahead of the pirate ships that marauded the coastline. He had heard them talking of *The Greek Fire* and they mentioned it with awe and fear. He watched them move along the bulwark towards the prow, then threw the sack onto his shoulder, grabbed a rope and jumped over the side, swinging as he did, so that his feet landed on the high deck wall of the neighbouring ship. Sorenson had left *the Long Serpent*.

He looked back and saw the three men deep in conversation. He left them to it. He hated to leave the ship. It had borne him well. But it was for the best. He sought out the two Varangian captains and told them that they must exchange ships.

- I am to become the Captain on board here. You two are to take my place.

- Both of us? To replace one man? It was the Icelander who spoke.

- General Sigurdsson has done with me. I am to follow his ship into battle; you two are to lead us now.

Beneath the serpent's head, Harald listened to the two Byzantine sailors, nodding. He smiled. And to himself he said:

- As for General Maniakes. I have plans for him.

HARALD HARDRADA - THE LAST VIKING

Georgios Maniakes had taken shelter much further north. He had had some success against the pirates and the Turks, and had laden his ships ready for the return to Constantinople. He knew that Empress Zoe would welcome him home, especially if he arrived there before her new favourite, the Varangian mercenary, Araltes. But news from the city was not good. If the news was to be believed – and his spies were reliable – then Emperor Michael was intent on taking all the power of the Empire to himself. He must show Zoe what she had always known. He, Georgios Maniakes, was her loyal and faithful servant and could be so much more. Now was the time to strike. Somewhere to the south, Araltes and the rest of the Varangians were holed up, waiting for this storm to pass. But he knew they were trapped. He had received word from the Norway Prince that Empress Zoe had sent for him, Araltes to ask his help in her battle against Michael. As soon as the storm was past, together they would sail to her rescue. Georgios Maniakes would not wait for the outsider. He would sail as soon as he could. Araltes was some days behind him, by which time...

Taking shelter on the island for a few days, Harald watched the two navigators as they concocted their recipe. He had wanted them to reveal its ingredients, but they refused, and he sensed that this was a matter of honour for them. Yes, they would make it for him, if they could gather the ingredients, but they could not share its secrets with him. He recognised naphtha oil and quicklime. But there were other ingredients too, not known to him. He would get it out of them eventually, but for now they must be left to the task. In five days they returned to the ship, with several barrels, full of black tarry liquid. The men cheered when the sail was raised. They'd spent too many days waiting and watching, from safe distance, the fleet of rebels that waited for them to emerge. He stood and watched the sail rise on its mast. The double-headed eagle would fly again, and no-one would stand in their way. The Varangian sailors had constructed the long pipes that had been drawn for them by the Byzantines. The nozzles were swung over the side of the ship, like a water hose. But it was not water that would be ejected. Harald had not told his men what would happen.

- *We have a secret weapon. Those pirates will get more than they bargained for.*

A cheer went up. And later when they saw the devastation – they shared none of Sorenson's reservations. They took delight, not only in setting fire to the onrushing ships, but aimed the fire across the water, boiling the bodies in the foaming sea. They marvelled at the way the fire seemed to float on water. None of them would forget the Greek Fire. The biggest cheer went up when the rest of the marauding fleet turned and fled. As they turned their ships northward, Sorenson's ship pulled alongside. The old captain stood watching his general. This was a man who would show no mercy. The City was three days' sail away. News reached them of the fate of Gyrgir. Maniakes had sailed into the awaiting arms of the usurper Emperor; his vessels sunk at Thessalonika. But if Harald had thought this would give him advantage...

The five ships hoisted white flags. They came in peace. The ships were allowed to sail through the Bosporus and saw the mighty gold domes and roofs. They moored alongside the city's warehouses. But there was a huge company of the Emperor's men waiting for them. And lengths of strong chains. Resistance would have been futile. Harald had a longer game to play.

HARALD HARDRADA - THE LAST VIKING

CHAINS

Harald Sigurdsson lay along the length of the bunk that was his bed. His blond head and his feet hung over the edges. The cell was clearly designed for smaller men. He listened to the rhythmic breathing of the old sailor, who fitted his bunk rather better.

- *Can you hear the noise, Sorenson?*

- *It sounds as if the people are in revolt.*

- *Is that a good thing, do you think?*

Sorenson's brain had been working hard. The riots had started the day before, but had intensified. Until then, there had been regular visits to the prison as rebels were rounded up and thrown in here to rot their lives away. Did the riots mean the rebels had now taken control? And what did it mean for them? He had hoped to die in his native land, not here in a foreign cell. It was not the empress who had incarcerated them. It was Michael, intent on preventing them sailing away with their hoarded treasures. There had been a pretence of a trial and they stood accused of stealing what was rightfully the emperor's. The fact that the empress was no longer able to stand witness to the contract she and Araltes had signed meant there was no-one to support them. No-one who dared oppose this usurper. The Varangian army had been defeated; those led by the upstart Maniakes had been killed. Destroyed at the harbour before they could enter the city, thanks to Sigurdsson's betrayal. But the old sailor knew he could expect no thanks. Emperor Michael knew what Harald planned. He too would be dealt with. Instead of a hero's welcome, Michael seized the ships and had them incarcerated beneath the city walls.

- *I had a dream last night, old man.*

HARALD HARDRADA - THE LAST VIKING

- Did it show you a way out of this place, a way out of Miklagard?

- I don't know what it meant. What do our dreams mean? Do they show us what is to be or what we would wish it to be?

- It's too deep for me, Sigurdsson.

- In my dream, I saw my brother, King Olaf, now a saint, all covered in white with a halo shining above his head.

- A saint indeed, then.

- He promised to help me escape.

- And do you believe these Christian visions, Sigurdsson?

- Like so many of us, Vikings, Sorenson, I carry a pagan heart and a Christian soul.

- So there is hope for us all... And did he say what would happen to your captain, my lord?

Harald ignored the sarcasm of the old sailor. He was used to it, and valued the man's honesty and his bravery. No-one else would dare to speak in that way. Good leaders needed wise councillors, and his hoary captain was certainly that.

- I was rescued by a lady of great distinction, dressed in the purple of the Empress...

- You think Zoe herself will turn the keys?

- Zoe is shut away. Michael has taken all the power to himself.

- Then she can be of little help to us.

They sat in silence for a while. They heard shouts outside, shouts of women and children. Their voices were close by. They were screaming out the empress's name.

The Varangians had rampaged through Jerusalem and they met with little resistance. It seemed as though the Arabs feared the damage that would ensue to their holy city and they retreated.

HARALD HARDRADA - THE LAST VIKING

Later the skald would write of those days:

> *Courage as keen as the weapon's edge,*
> *Was this warrior's sword.*
> *And the land gave up its holy sites,*
> *Undisputed and unseared.*
> *And in the holy Jordan river,*
> *He bathed as pilgrims must.*
> *In this way did Harald celebrate*
> *A victory for Christ.*

On Harald's return from Jerusalem, he had found Constantinople in chaos. The emperor had taken more and more power to himself, despite the fact that it was Zoe who had been born "into the purple". Harald and his men were eager to return North, to wrest the title of King of Norway from his nephew, who now had dominion over Denmark as well as Norway. He saw his chance to at last take on the role he was made for, the one promised him by his sainted brother.

Perhaps because of her title as Porphyrogenita, Michael had not attempted to assassinate her, but had her imprisoned in a nunnery, under lock and key and an armed guard, loyal to him. Harald and his Varangian guard were loyal to Zoe, and made an attempt to overthrow the emperor, but they had been rounded up and imprisoned. He assumed they were still alive only because Michael believed they could be ransomed for a princely sum from Jaroslav. They were held in the fortress, and awaited their fate. He had been allowed – encouraged – to write to The Grand Duke, and Harald had told the Rus leader how things stood. There had been no reply, but perhaps Michael had intercepted the letters from Kiev. Michael was well aware that Araltes's loyalty lay with the Empress.

Harald remembered the eve of her banishment. He was brought into her presence, and he saw they were alone, for the first time.

- *So Araltes. Jerusalem has fallen and We are supreme again.*

- *I have done all a man can do to serve the Empress.*

- *You have indeed, General. And you have spared that great city from fire and sword.*

- *And now, I would beg leave to return home. There are battles to be fought in my own lands, Empress.*

- *We are not ready to release you yet.*

Harald was dismayed. He had hoped that Zoe would release him from his vow of obedience.

- *Have I not served the Empire well? I ask only in return to be released from my contract.*

- *I have a new contract in mind.*

Harald's mind raced. Back in Kiev, Jaroslav and Harald had laid plans. He would marry Anastasia - Harald had admired the blond-haired beauty - and take the title Emperor in any way he could. But Anastasia was gone, to Hungary. Perhaps the dark-haired Elisiv was still free. He knew she wanted him. But, Jaroslav had made it clear: he should do whatever it took to bring the Empire closer to the Rus; he, Harald, would rule it for him with one of Jaroslav's own daughters. The time was coming for Jaroslav to reap the rewards of sheltering the displaced princes. Anastasia had gone to Hungary, and Agatha may well marry England's next king. Now Harald wondered if the time had come, in different circumstances. Zoe was offering more than he dared hope. She wanted to marry him. Michael would follow her first husband into the ground. Perhaps she wanted him, her Araltes, to do the deed.

HARALD HARDRADA - THE LAST VIKING

But Zoe's husbands had a habit of dying prematurely. And there were other ways to assume power, playing a longer game.

- *What did the Empress have in mind? A marriage to her niece, Maria, perhaps?*

-*Maria? No. she is not for you Araltes. For you, I have someone else in mind. Someone much higher born.*

Harald felt the ground shifting beneath his feet. He was at her mercy and he needed something...

- *The Empress honours me. But I must tell her that I am betrothed.*

Twice over, he thought. Jaroslav had hinted strongly that he was to marry his daughter. And there had been Torah too...

He thought of Torah now, in his cell... The beautiful girl of his youth, who had come to him naked in the night during one of his visits back home. They had spent a night together, a night that made his loins ache to remember. And she was an Arnason; daughter to one of the most powerful earls in Norway. She was his way back to the throne. Even while Magnus ruled with the help of other Earls, it was Harald's throne, promised to him, and he would fight the boy-king, the bastard boy, for the right to fulfil his destiny.

Torah, Elisiv and Zoe... But Michael stood in their way. They stood accused of treason and the emperor feared them.

- *Someone is coming, Prince. I hear women's voices and there are keys rattling in cages.*

- *Let us hope they come to release us... And that Michael is no longer ruling the Empire.*

The keys in the lock turned and the door swung open. Beyond the threshold the corridor was crowded with women.

HARALD HARDRADA - THE LAST VIKING

- Follow us, Araltes. Follow us. Escape and rescue our beloved Empress. Michael is dead, Zoe must be returned to us.

Harald and Sorenson needed no further prompting. They followed where the ladies led. Up, up, up. Then they emerged onto the flat roof of the parapet. The Varangian guards were ready for him, and already below were his captains, Ulf and Halldor. Ropes had been lowered and they scrambled below, to where more men and women from the city waited for him, Araltes, to rescue their Empress. They made their way over dead bodies that lay where they had fallen; they passed more bodies hanging from the city walls. The Golden City had become blood red.

> **He who had fed the carrion crows**
> **Tore the eyes from Michael's head.**
> **Miklagard restored to its former state.**
> **Another Emperor lay dead.**

Harald stole into the royal apartments before Zoe had been fetched back, where he found what he was searching for, and carried it away to where ships lay waiting for him. The Varangians had prepared two ships for flight. Men were ready at the oars and both ships were being loosed from their moorings as he boarded with his bundle. Unlike in his beloved Northern lands, night-time in Constantinople was never black. Lights shone out across the waters from the city walls. But this would be no easy journey through the Bosporus. It was Ulf Ospaksson who asked the question:

- What will do now, Prince? How will we escape the iron chains that stretch across the harbour?

- I have a plan, Ulf. And they spoke quietly together.

The boats rowed smoothly and quietly, oars pulling deep to keep the noise down. They saw the chain ahead of them. It was a

HARALD HARDRADA - THE LAST VIKING

fearsome sight, and one that had kept the city safe; frightening pirates trying to gain entry, and merchantmen trying to leave without paying the taxes due. Now it was ready to destroy the boats of the fleeing Varangians and their treasure. The chains grew in size as they made the entrance to the Sound, and they glistened in the light of a full moon. At his signal, half the men released their oars and raced to the back of the ship with everything they could grab in their hands. Their momentum and weight lifted the bow up; as it passed the line of chain, they were ordered to the bow, and the stern lifted out of the water. They had crossed the chain. The oarsmen slackened off and a great cheer went out, but it died on their lips as they saw the second ship had not made it. Its bow raised up, but sank again before it crossed the chain. They herd the metallic thud as the keel split, and they watched as their companions sank to the bottom of the Bosporus. Harald had lost his Captain. Sorenson was dead, and all the crew, their bodies rising to bob, lifeless on the water. No journey home awaited them. No heroes' welcome. Harald would miss the hoary sage. How differently it might have ended for him if they had not quarrelled over the sea-fire.

The mood was solemn when they resumed their journey northwards. But Harald ordered the crew to pull over alongside an island wharf. There he unwrapped his bundle and to the astonishment of all, out stepped Maria.

- *Tell your Aunt, Empress Zoe, that she has no hold over me. Her power doesn't reach so far and had I so chosen, you, Maria, would have been my bride.*

During the journey he searched amongst his treasure for two special pieces that he'd set aside for gifts to Anastasia, which would now be sent to Elisiv. With this bronze cross and gold ring he sent verses of love which ended with a simple question:

HARALD HARDRADA - THE LAST VIKING

Will the Goddess in Russia
Accept my gold tokens?

But Harald did not stop there. He sent another ring to Norway, to the Arnasons. And a simple message:

In honour of my contract with Torah, I am
returning home to claim my throne.

Harald saw his destiny as King of Norway. It had been promised him; and he would take every opportunity to fulfil that destiny. The future might be complicated but he would let it take care of itself.

HARALD HARDRADA - THE LAST VIKING

BRIDES

His ship bobbed on the icy blue sea. It seemed to Harald that all of Novgorod stood there at the wharf to welcome him. The story of his escape from Miklagard had preceded him, and Jaroslav had moved the court north to greet his Varangians.

- So, Prince Harald returns. Chains cannot hold you.

- No-one can hold me, Grand Duke. But we mourn our losses. Good men were sunk in the Hellespont that day.

- I have a special visitor for you.

In truth, Harald had already spotted her. The raven-haired princess stood by her father's side. Elisiv may have lacked Anastasia's beauty, but she lacked nothing of her sister's heritage. She was he father's eldest daughter and would be expected to make a good marriage. She was already past the usual age where such contracts have been drawn up. He remembered the conversation he and Ulf Ospaksson had had, standing together beneath the serpent's head prow.

- Elisiv of Kiev will make a better wife for you. She is a feisty girl, suited to your wild nature, Harald. She is the granddaughter of a Swedish King as well as the daughter of a Rus Emperor. And beside she has the keys to Novgorod – her father's gift – and the keys to Novgorod will open your treasury.

Ulf Ospaksson was no fool. He was not an expert in wiving, but he knew politics. A marriage to Elisiv would be a good contract. Jaroslav spread his arms wide and the party opened up, revealing, behind him, his daughter. And Harald was smitten. Her face was an open book. In it Harald could read the story of this young woman. She was more than ten years his junior, and at the age of nineteen, she was much more of a woman than he'd remembered. How much better then, that this political alliance would also be a thing of pleasure. He looked for her hand, but they were tucked tightly into her woollen muffler. Was she wearing his ring?

- Welcome, Prince Harald. Welcome home to Rus.

- My home is Norway, Princess.

- My mother is a Princess. Alas, I am merely the eldest daughter of a Grand Duke. And she smiled at him, and her father smiled too.

- But you will become a Queen, if you will accept me.

- I was bewitched by your poetry, Prince. But is the man who writes such fancy words, a man to rule a kingdom?

She looked hard into his face, seeing again the livid scar that marked this warrior. Harald smiled, and he saw the effect that he had upon her. She smiled again and it seemed to him that the sun burned brighter. All thoughts of Anastasia were gone.

- Fancy words exalt our deeds, Elisiv. It is words that keep you alive long after your body is dust.

- Then, with my father's permission I shall wear your gift. She withdrew her hands and held the ring in her palm.

Jaroslav stepped between them.

- My daughter is a prize greater than all your wealth, Prince of Norway. But she is to be married to a King, not a Prince.

- Then give her to me, Jaroslav. For together we shall rule both Denmark and Norway. And my people will love her. And the Rus and the Vikings will live in peace.

- But Magnus is King in Norway. I myself released him into Einar Thambarskelfir's care. And now, by Harthacnut's death, he is King of Denmark too.

- Magnus is not my brother's true heir. And with Elisiv by my side I shall return to Norway to claim my birthright.

And she stood by his side, gave him the ring with her hand outstretched, and Harald slid it onto her finger.

> *The Viking Warrior King*
> *Fought and won the soul*
> *Of his royal-bloodied mistress*
> *A treasure more than gold.*

And they were married in the Winter.

Far away in the frozen lands of Norway, Torah Torbergsdotter received the news calmly. Torah did everything calmly. It was her nature. But beneath the calm, her heart was beating fast and her blood was boiling. She had been called to her uncle's farmstead, in Austrått. Finn Arnason was livid.

- How dare he treat us like this? Does he not know who he insults? It was we who kept him safe. It was we who helped him south to Jaroslav. And now he does this.

- No contract was made, Uncle.

- You and he slept together. That is his contract. And now he thinks he can marry a Rus Princess and bring her back to be Queen of Norway – and Denmark too?

- But it is done, Finn. It was Kalfr who spoke, Finn's younger brother. *– And with it he has shown himself to have no loyalty to us. You were father to the boy, taught him the arts of war, long before Olaf returned. And we swore to support his claim to the throne. But now...*

Torah watched them. These were the men who really controlled the power throughout the Kingdom. If Harald was to return to be King of Norway, he could only do so with their support. With their blessing.

HARALD HARDRADA - THE LAST VIKING

- No contract was made, Uncle. He has a wife. And we are too late. That ship has sailed.

Finn took her by the shoulders and looked her squarely in the face.

- He will not be the first king to have two wives.

- It is forbidden, Uncle.

- Who forbids what I allow?

- God forbids.

- Norwegians have followed their own laws long before God came to these shores. It is not too late. I shall hold Harald to his promise.

And with that they were gone, and she was left to herself. They were right of course. While nothing had been said, nothing sworn, Harald was to wed her, Torah, not some Rus Princess. And if he had broken that vow then it was her, the Rus, who was no wife to Harald. *She* was the illegitimate bride, marrying a man already betrothed. But how would she put it right? They were coming here, to Norway. Harald and Elisiv of Rus. They were coming to claim a kingdom, and how did she fit into that scheme?

In the spring, the ships were ready to sail. The Varangian fleet stood in the harbour on Lake Ladoga, and Elisiv stood with him, her hand in his. This fleet would take her to her new country where together they would rule. She had longed for this day. As a child she knew she was destined for adventures; knew she was meant to travel beyond Kiev, beyond Rus. And here she was, on the brink of an adventure like no other. With a husband like no other.

Things had moved so quickly. After their wedding they had stayed in Novgorod, together emptying the exchequer. The treasures that Harald had amassed in Italy and Constantinople would be put to good use. An army had been assembled and ships had been built. And now he would lead her to her destiny. But not until they had spent nights together. That first night: she remembered the strength of his body, holding her tight and exploring her. She pushed the initial pain aside and then clung on to him and they stayed locked together. And as night followed day, they grew closer. And her body began to change. And she shared the secret with him and they laughed together. This boy would be his heir. She had been afraid at first that Harald would sleep apart from her, as so many husbands did when their wives conceived. But not *her* husband. He held her close, as if he couldn't bear to be parted from her, and from the tiny son that she bore. She moved closer to him. She had something for him, a parting gift from her father which she was to present to him at this very moment. She called forward her servant, and snapped her fingers impatiently. The servant produced the rolled cloth. She untied the knots that kept it rolled and handed it to her husband. How she enjoyed that – her husband.

- I have a gift for you. From my father.

- He has already given me the best gift I could have.

Harald took the roll of cloth and, laying it onto the wooden pier he unrolled it. Slowly it revealed itself. Here was a flag to put fear into any heart. The black raven. The raven that was the 'landwaster', feeding off the carcases left in battle, but the raven was also the wise bird of Thor himself. Here was a potent symbol, and one of great portent.

The cold spring seemed a long way off to her. Here, still in her father's kingdom, still the daughter of a Grand Duke, Elisiv grew impatient. It was north and west her future lay. Plans were being laid; messengers were sent back and forth. It soon became clear to her that the return to Norway would not be a glorious one. Though her husband did not share affairs of state with her, it was from her father that she heard what awaited her.

 - *There will be a battle. Magnus will not give up his claim on the throne as easily as Harald may have imagined.*

- *He is a boy, father. Harald will crush him.*

- *But the boy has something precious. He bears the love of both peoples. The Danes welcome him as a kind and gentle ruler; the Norwegians love him for his sainted father's sake.*

Elisiv sucked on her bottom lip. She knew her father spoke the truth. Harald was a warrior. The men had a name for him – "Hardrada". She thought of him as a man of "stern counsel", but knew that the word had other meanings, some much crueller. He was not a man to be universally loved, but one to be admired for his resolve, his strength of purpose and for his clear-sightedness. If Harald set his mind on something nothing would shift him. In this he was more like her father; to become king was not to win a popularity contest. But she knew that Magnus held all the cards. When she shared her fears with him he reassured her:

- *Magnus is my nephew. He is the son of my brother, and he knows what it will cost him to stand against me. For now, he has all the earls with him, but I have plans to draw them away from him.*

- *He has two kingdoms now; surely he can spare one for his uncle?*

And Harald smiled at this. Elisiv thought about the young Magnus she recalled from his early days in exile in her father's court.

- *I remember how good a boy he was. Always willing to share.*

- *As a boy, Elisiv, I refused to share anything. When the time comes, it is we who shall set the terms, not the bastard boy.*

HARALD HARDRADA - THE LAST VIKING

And she watched his retreating back, broad and unyielding. She was afraid that it would take much time - and blood before she wore a crown on her head.

The preparations filled the late spring and early summer days. Then at last they were ready, and as the ships grew, so did Elisiv. The baby boy grew inside her. But to what lands would he become heir? At last the day came. She had spent the final days with her parents in Kiev. She had left her husband reluctantly; he had insisted that she give proper farewells to her family. He owed much to Jaroslav.

- *We shall not leave like thieves in the night. Who knows when we shall return?*

So Elisiv stayed at the palace, enjoying her time with her siblings as well as her parents. Anastasia, too was making plans to move. She and Andrew had been married over five years, but his claim to the throne of Hungary had been challenged and now he waited while rebels sympathetic to the young exile stirred up wars. In that they were supported by Jaroslav and his troops. Her father had much to gain from having a son-in-law King of Hungary. And now he was close to being called. Elisiv couldn't help but feel jealous of her older sister. She was already a mother; her daughter Adelaide, as a girl, was not a strong guarantee of the future, but Elisiv watched mother and child enviously, remembering her own relationship with her mother. She was more concerned that it now seemed as if Anastasia would become a queen before she did. They would all be queens one day: Anastasia; Anne, betrothed to the exiled Henry of France; and Agatha, the youngest of them who ran around the palace in the company of the English Prince Edward. The Rus palace was full of promises. But for now it was her destiny that filled the air. Her goodbyes were painfully sweet. She would miss them all, even

HARALD HARDRADA - THE LAST VIKING

Anastasia with her beautiful hair, so like their mothers. And it was her mother most of all she would miss. She spent those last days hanging on her arm and on her words, milking for all she could these memories that may have to last her a lifetime.

At the end of summer, she returned to Ladoga, and together she and her husband sailed west to Sweden, to the port at Sigtuna. They had been at sea only two weeks, before Elisiv's labour pains began. When they arrived in Sweden, they arrived as a family of three. If Harald was disappointed that his first-born was a daughter, he didn't say as much to Elisiv.

- Our daughter is so beautiful, Elisiv. She will make a fine Viking princess.

And Elisiv agreed. Her daughter had the beautiful fair hair of her grandmother and her aunt Stasie, but which had bypassed her. Harald had seen the likeness too. He had held her under the stars, washed by spray, and named her Ingegerd.

- Because she is so like your mother, Elisiv, she shall be given her name. May she grow as wise and as beautiful.

And Elisiv loved Harald even more for the gesture.

- And may she make as good a marriage as I have, Harald.

And they kissed under the stars.

- They have a child now, uncle. Does that not make matters even worse? Even harder?

- They have a daughter, niece. You will give him sons.

News of Harald's arrival at Sigtuna was everywhere. After five years of fighting for peace, no-one wanted more war, unless of course it brought more power to the earls at Giske, and Finn Arnason was determined to gather up more power to himself.

HARALD HARDRADA - THE LAST VIKING

What better way than to offer support to Harald? In return Torah would become his legitimate queen, betrothed long before he married the Rus girl. And when Torah gave him sons, all would be complete.

- I feel I know her already, Uncle Finn, this Elisiv of Kiev.

- Have you met her? Finn was concerned that she lacked the ambition.

- No. But news of her is everywhere. Did you know that she and I were born in the same year? And there are pictures too, cut into woodblocks with runes of praise around her. Runes that Harald himself has cast in her honour. They speak of her "raven-black hair", her "dark eyes", her "slim figure", even after the baby. Elisiv is beautiful.

- And you too are beautiful, niece. And you will beguile him. The stories I heard were that he really wanted to marry the older sister, Anastasia. She has long blond hair, like yours; she has eyes the colour of the fjords, as you do. When he sees you, he will regret and forget his marriage to the raven. He will remember his promise.

And Torah wrapped her arms around herself, imagining them to be his arms, imagining herself to be his wife. Imagining herself to be Queen of Norway.

HARALD HARDRADA - THE LAST VIKING

PACTS

Elisiv knew her destiny: she would be Queen of Norway. Elisiv felt safe in Sweden. From here she would march alongside her husband to their palace in the north. Sweden felt like home to Harald, too. It had the same rugged coastline and steep-sided fjords of his native land; and more importantly it was a land where he felt safe, under the protection of his family. And not only *his* family. Elisiv, too could trace her family back to this land; the late king Olaf Eiriksson, was her mother's grandfather. Here they would live under the protection of King Anund Jacob. Here they could prepare their strategies. Here they could rest awhile, and let their baby girl grow up strong. But the shadow of war was darkening their days. Less than a week after they had landed, before she had even had a chance to gain her land-legs, Sveyn Ulfsson arrived. From that first encounter, Elisiv knew the man was trouble. He was a tall man, shaggy-haired, and despite his being five years Harald's junior, he looked older. He had a limp; had had it since childhood, a birth defect. In her eyes it made him less of a man; more like a wounded bear. The two men had met and talked in private for several hours. Then Sveyn was dispatched.

- *What did he want?*

- *Sveyn and I have made a pact.*

- *What sort of pact?*

- *We shall go to war with Magnus, and take back from him the lands that were promised to me.*

- *Can he be trusted, this Ulfsson?*

- *No man can be trusted, Elisiv. But we have mutual interests. And he is a cousin by marriage. So he is family.*

HARALD HARDRADA - THE LAST VIKING

- *Magnus is family too. Would it not be better to make peace with him?*

- *Sveyn tried that and met only war.*

Elisiv tried to remember the young Magnus who had stayed in her father's court at Kiev when he fled from conquered Norway, after the death of his father. She hadn't thought of him as a warrior.

- *Who would have thought of Magnus as a fighter?*

- *It is not him who leads the struggle but the earls who keep him on the thrones. He is still a green boy, barely twenty and he rules over both countries, Denmark and Norway.*

- *And how will a pact with Sveyn help? The man has proven himself a weak leader. He has lost battle after battle to the boy Magnus.*

Harald took their daughter from her arms. His eyes were firmly fixed ahead of him, those steely cool blue eyes, the colour of the fjord waters.

- *By the time this one is able to walk, you and I, Elisiv, will be King and Queen of both countries. But for now we need Sveyn. He has a loyal following here in Sweden. And beyond, in Norway, he has the support of the northern earls of Giske. If I can win their support, we shall fulfil our destiny. We shall deal first with Magnus, and then with Sveyn.*

Elisiv took baby Inge and held her tight.

- *I don't trust the man. Sveyn wants power and he needs us more than we need him.*

And Harald looked at her, and he smiled. He knew what he had married; a warrior queen, one who was fit to stand by his side. And she felt closer to him.

- *We have shaken hands on it, Elisiv. But what is a handshake worth when set against our destiny?*

HARALD HARDRADA - THE LAST VIKING

And she smiled, seeing her father's ruthlessness in her husband. He was a man fated to be a great ruler; and she was a woman to stand by him.

Two days later, messengers from King Magnus arrived. They sued for peace offering a share of the kingdoms. And a clear message of warning.

- I won all of Denmark on Harthacnut's death because I had the support of their chieftains. Your name however, only raises fear. I have reconciled myself with my father's enemies. All across Norway and Denmark I am called Magnus the Good. It will take more than your treasure and the armies it buys to prise these kingdoms away.

They were sent back with a clear message. War was coming.

The ocean parted,
Sea-spray rained.
Your mighty ships
With blood were stained.
To Danish isles
From Sweden's shore
The driving storms,
To battle bore.
Weak and trembling hearts;
Behold your raven sails.
Your destiny awaits you.
An enemy's courage fails.

HARALD HARDRADA - THE LAST VIKING

Elisiv listened to the news that came on the tide.

My dearest Queen – for I shall give your proper title – how does my little Princess fare?

Zealand has fallen, and Fyn is crushed. Buildings burn, but the people are spared. These Danes may not love me, but let them taste my mercy as well as my anger. The name Hardrada is feared everywhere but they know I can be merciful...

Sveyn's ships look more terrifying than they are but the man himself inspires more fear than love. He has little prowess but he is useful. Magnus has returned to Norway and sues for peace...

Elisiv had heard as much herself. King Magnus – now universally called "The Good" had been advised not to take up arms against Harald. They were both kinsmen of the sainted Olaf, and no good could come of their fighting.

...I have accepted his terms; a half-share in the Kingdom of Norway...

Elisiv held up her hand to put the words aside. Did that make her half a queen; her daughter half a princess? What was Harald thinking?

...and equal shares of our combined wealth. We are rich beyond measure, my Queen.

Elisiv dismissed the couriers. "Rich beyond measure"? that was not her dream. News had come to her from Anastasia. She and Andrew now ruled in Hungary. And her other sisters were destined for crowns and thrones. They were not given shares in kingdoms. Magnus made fun of them. While he held a kingdom and a half, Harald, his uncle, the legitimate heir, would have just half of Norway! How could Harald do this to her?

HARALD HARDRADA - THE LAST VIKING

Sveyn was furious with Harald. He had come to meet with him between battles on the Danish isles. Sveyn knew of the pact that had been signed between Magnus and Harald. Elisiv could barely bring herself to greet him. The two men sat together at the head of the table, with Elisiv at her husband's side. She listened to the talk that flowed between them, both barely able to contain the hatred each felt for the other. Sveyn felt betrayed.

- Of all the things I treasure most, it is the banner, given to me by my wife. The Landwaster.

- And what makes this banner so treasured, cousin?

- It brings victory to the man who follows it into battle. That is certainly what it has done for me.

- I will believe in its power when you have fought and won three battles against Magnus.

Elisiv smiled to herself. Sveyn sought to break the pact between Magnus and Harald, and while she was not happy with it, she would prefer her husband to be separate from Sveyn. She trusted Magnus more than this "wounded bear".

- You only honour the pledges that benefit you, Harald. You will betray any man that stands between you and power.

It was Elisiv who cut into the growing anger that bristled around the table:

- My husband has broken his pledges fewer times than you have done with King Magnus, my lord Sveyn. And she smiled her winning smile at the shaggy giant.

Later, in their rooms, Harald berated her.

- These are affairs of state, Elisiv. I know the man is not to be trusted. But we can ill-afford to make an enemy of him while he has so many men at his disposal. He is likely to murder us both in our beds.

- Then we best be prepared, Harald...

HARALD HARDRADA - THE LAST VIKING

They came at night. The splash of oars was muffled, and the small boat drew alongside the harbour wall and two men, dressed in black to hide them in the night, crept into the bedchamber. Only their axes shone in the starlight. They raised the weapons high above the bed and chopped and slashed at the bodies that lay there. Just as quickly they were gone.

Sveyn Ulfsson stood at the prow of his ship. With Harald dead, he would assume total charge of the armies. Up until now Magnus had been a difficult enemy; he was well-supported and well-loved. He knew what the Viking warriors said of his own leadership. *A man who wins no battles can never be king.* He had felt undermined by Harald, who challenged his authority even with his own men. But that was no longer a problem. Harald was dead, and with him, his wife, the Kiev witch, who showed him, Sveyn, scant regard. When the messenger came, as he knew he would, he would feign surprise...

- My lord Ulfsson...

- What is it? Do you bring me good news or bad?

- I don't know my lord.

- To whom does it relate?

- To my lord Sigurdsson, the Prince Harald.

Sveyn tried to suppress the smile but he could feel the corners of his mouth turning up.

- What of him?

- He has gone, my lord.

- Gone? You mean dead?

- Not dead my lord Ulfsson. Gone. His ships have sailed.

- And he is aboard?

HARALD HARDRADA - THE LAST VIKING

- Yes, my lord.

Sveyn clenched his teeth. Harald Sigurdsson had tricked him. Well, let him go, cap in hand to Norway. Denmark will be lost to him forever.

- And even now, he sails towards Magnus's ships with a white flag.

They stood together beneath the prow of the ship. The raven banner had been furled and the white flags flew hard and straight. Magnus would not mistake their purpose. The ships docked, and Harald, with Elisiv beside him, went to meet his nephew. Even before they arrived, it was clear that Magnus was waiting for them, but not in ambush. In welcome.

- Uncle. It is good to see you. I have waited for this day. You have seen the treacherous Sveyn for what he is. He wants power only for himself. His constant warring has caused too many deaths, too much pain in our kingdom, and we want peace. More than anything, in the name of our beloved Saint Olaf, we want peace.

- And we are here, nephew, to make peace.

And the two kinsmen hugged. Elisiv watched the two men, bound by their blood.

Later in their rooms, she asked:

- And what of us, Harald? What is to become of us? Are we to be kinsmen of a king, and no more? And will our daughter, born to be a princess, never fulfil her destiny.

- We are agreed, Magnus and I. Norway shall have two kings. And Sveyn shall keep Denmark.

- And I shall be half a queen?

- You will be queen, Elisiv. And our children will be heirs, for Magnus has no wife and no children to stake their claim. It's a

long game to play, and Magnus is a sickly man; he lacks his father's
strength...
- And his uncle's cunning.

> **Distant travel has made you wise;**
> **And now your return is marked in honour.**
> **Norway now divides in peace,**
> **And both your treasures bestowed upon her.**
> **When royal clansmen met**
> **Great cheering rent the air.**
> **Together they would rule the land**
> **An inheritance to share.**

It was late at night, when Magnus appeared in his uncle's tent.
Elisiv was in the shadows feeding Ingegerd at her breast. She felt
hidden.

- So uncle. I bring you lots to draw. But I have heard the stories of
you and lots... this time I hope you will be straight.

- And what will be determined by this draw?

The men spoke quietly, but above the quiet sucking baby breaths,
Elisiv heard.

- We shall divide up our power between us. It matters not which
you choose. Only that you choose to draw.

Elisiv looked at Magnus, and remembered the bookish boy who
had spent his childhood hidden from Cnut's swords, in her father's
Kiev palace. He had grown wiser. And she saw Harald draw the
straw and the two men held each other tight, hands and forearms
clutched tight. She was to be queen. But as Magnus spoke she
heard the terms.

- These straws are a symbol of our pact. You shall be king as
lawfully as I over every part of Norway. But...

She felt the mood change in that instant. She saw the set of Harald's jaw.

- ... when we are together, I am to be accorded precedence; in harbour I shall have the royal berth. And in return you are to support and strengthen our kingdom. And our treasure shall be divided equally.

- I agree to the terms and swear my allegiance, nephew.

Elisiv and Harald were already prepared for such terms. Much of his treasure had been set aside and lay hidden elsewhere. But the terms were poor ones. Half a queen, then. A royal only in name. This was not enough.

A messenger from far away to the North in Austrått, carried a letter from Finn Arnason. It was clear that Magnus was not the king the Giske family had chosen. Sveyn had promised them more. It seemed that his power-base was eroding. The only hope was that Harald would be true to the promise he made to Torah. And as Magnus had no children, it would be Torah's children that would inherit. The marriage to the Rus woman would be null and void, he claimed. He addressed Harald as the half-king.

- Harald, come north to visit us. There is much we can do to help you. If your nephew should meet with an accident – for word is he is a feeble man – than your power would double. And you will need the Giske family to tear Denmark from Sveyn's grip. For Norway and Denmark should stay together. You will remember Torah, my niece, to whom you are still betrothed. She would welcome you here as much as I would. And if what I hear is true, that your Rus princess cannot give you boys, then perhaps the future lies with

Torah? In return for such a visit perhaps we can find ways of making you twice the man you are now!

Harald shared only some of its contents with Elisiv. Torah's part in the pact were hidden from her.

- Will he rid of us the bastard?

- I think he offers it.

- And what does he want in return?

- More power to the Giske earls.

Elisiv smelt a rat, but could not see the treachery.

- And is he to be trusted?

- No-one is to be trusted, Elisiv. But if his actions give us all of Norway...

Harald carefully composed his reply and sent it northwards.

In Ringerike, Brenn and Dag, heard the news. So, at last, after sixteen years, Harald had inherited his father's throne, shared with the bastard boy Magnus. Brenn was old now. She had waited for this day, to see *her boy* achieve the destiny his youth had promised. As night fell, Dag returned to the farmhouse.

- And what difference will it make to our lives, mother? What difference does any of this make to our lives. It is like a game of tafel. And we are little more than pawns in the game.

- You will see, Dag. He will send for you, to be at his side. He will remember his boyhood days at Ringerike. He will remember the sacrifices made at Stikelstad. He will send for you.

- And will I go?

- Of course you will go. He is your brother.

- He has forgotten his playmate, his comrade-in-arms. He has sailed across Southern seas and he will have long-forgotten us.

- No. It is not so. A man never forgets his home. And Harald will pay his debt to you. You will see. He will come.

When news of Magnus's death came, Elisiv donned black, but her heart was light. At last she was Queen; Norway was hers, and her beautiful daughter, now learning to walk and talk, would inherit the kingdom. As it was always meant to be.

> *The death of a good king is a heavy burden.*
> *Courtiers struck with grief; eyes wet with tears.*
> *His people would mourn this good king for ever;*
> *His name and deeds endure well into future years.*

1066

HARALD HARDRADA - THE LAST VIKING

ST MATTHEW'S DAY. From our positions on the ridge above the city walls, we can see the army encampment. Behind them the walls of the city stand firm. The gates will be closed, I know, but they will not be able to resist us. Earl Edwin sits astride his horse, the flag of St George flapping wildly in the wind. I watch as they ready themselves. But what is to follow will catch them unawares. They cannot imagine what force will hit them.

Harald has prepared his fighting positions. At the front, the first wave will be led by Tostig. He has the support of the local army and is driven by revenge upon his brother Harold. Harald holds himself in reserve, and I sit astride my horse in the lines behind my king. Suddenly the sun emerges and with it comes the first charge. We watch as Tostig's men repulse the first wave, but slowly, Edwin's men make ground against them. Now it is our turn. We move forward, foot soldiers ahead of a line of mounted men. We are Vikings and fighting is in our nature. The English soldiers who follow Tostig are farmers, and the art of warfare is not in their blood. We drive through the retreating army, and push Edwin's men back northwards, towards the city's walls. Wave after wave of the English soldiers come at us, but they cannot break our shield wall. They should have stayed hidden behind their thick stone walls, but they underestimate us. They underestimate our king. He has made a promise to his queen. She will sit alongside him on the English throne and this promise drives him on.

We push them back, and rush into the opening their dead men leave. Men and hooves climb over fallen English bodies, and the city stands unguarded before us. Behind me I hear the fires that wait to be used to destroy the city. The heat sears my back. We are going to set fire to Jorvik. Nothing will be left of this mighty city inside its stone walls. The first arrows hit their mark and a cheer goes up as we watch the smoke plume above the walls.

And suddenly, Edwin himself sits astride his horse, the city gates behind him. Harald rides to meet him. And they sit side by side. The talking is finished, and Harald turns to us, holding a key aloft. The city has surrendered. The fires will go hungry. Jorvik is ours.

1047 - 1051

Farmers, already feasted on blood,
Set themselves for war again,
To face the ships and warriors
Of the bellicose king of Danes.
Only God Himself will know
Which will live, which will not;
One king will rob the other
Of all his lands, his life, his lot.
King Harald sailed in anger
Vessels armed for war;
Not satisfied with Norway's crown,
He hungered now for more.

HARALD HARDRADA - THE LAST VIKING

CAPITAL

- *Kings and Queens should live in palaces, and princesses too.*

It had been a thorn between them every day since Harald had become undisputed king of Norway. He had told Elisiv:

- *It is not the Norwegian way to live in a stone palace. We build in wood and our grand halls are as palatial as any...*

But Elisiv remembered her life in Kiev, in her father's palace, and she wanted her daughter to live the life she had lived.

- *Besides,* she said, *who is to say what is and what isn't? Norway has a new royal family. We can make the rules.*

Harald saw the legacy such a building would bring. For some weeks now they had set up camp on a small port on the River Alna. It was close to his boyhood home at Ringerike. And, more importantly, from there he could stretch his hands across the sea to Denmark, where Sveyn had set himself up as king, in defiance of the natural laws. He, Harald, was Magnus's nearest relative; he, Harald, had the rights of inheritance. And he, Harald would drive Sveyn out of Denmark.

- *Here would be a perfect spot.*

Elisiv stood on the dockside, where wooden jetties rotted in the water.

- *Build a new city, build a palace fit for a King of Norway. Show the rebel Danes how powerful you are. No-one will ever dare to defy such a mighty king. Resistance will crumble.*

Harald smiled at his wife. She knew which buttons to press, which levers to pull. And she was right. Now that he was King of Norway, why should he not live in the grand manner, like Jaroslav in Kiev. He would build a city to rival the Rus capital. A city from where mighty ships would sail and conquer. A city where his heirs would grow up knowing what it was to be powerful.

141

HARALD HARDRADA - THE LAST VIKING

It was the thought of his heirs that made him fretful. They had prayed for a boy, and when the prayers were answered but he died before he drew breath, they extended their prayers. But to no avail. Elisiv blamed the cold rooms in their wooden manor house.

- *Once we have a comfortable palace, childbirth will be easier for me. We shall have a boy, you shall see. He is waiting to be born in a palace.*

And Harald held her tight, and prayed again.

The city grew slowly but it was a good place to be. Here, the air was milder, even in the harsh winters, so much further south. Not as far south as her beloved Kiev, she knew, but with the ocean so close, it felt gentler and softer on her skin. Surely if *she* felt good, it would be a better place to give birth to the son she knew Harald wanted; the son that Norway needed. And each day she watched as the palace grew.

Harald started his new city from the river, from where it was easier to defend. Sveyn continued to defy him. He had even sent raiding parties to destroy docks and ships further round the coast. Harald chased him, but he always managed to escape. Today, with the docks now complete, Harald would bring his fleet south to the city and they would set out to teach the false Danish King a lesson, one that would end in his death. With Ulf Ospaksson he walked its length, admiring the berths and fortifications that protected them. Harald looked out to the mouth of the channel:

- *Perhaps we too should erect chains to stop any invading fleet.*

Ulf took his arm and turned him to face the hills that overlooked the growing city. He pointed up at them.

- *We have no need of such methods, Harald. We have natural fortifications. No ship will come through to these docks unless we have agreed it should pass.*

HARALD HARDRADA - THE LAST VIKING

Harald turned his back on the water and looked northward, to where the walls of the palace grew.

- *Is this no more than vanity, Ulf Ospaksson?*

- *What is a king if not a vanity, Harald? And a queen has a right to feel safe.*

- *I think she misses home. She gets messages every week, from Kiev, telling her news of her sisters.*

Elisiv had shown him the latest of these, but he found it hard to read the Rus script.

- *Tell me what they say, Elisiv.*

- *It is news of Agatha and Ann. Agatha has married her Prince Edward and they have sailed to England to stake his claim to the throne.*

And not for the first time Harald felt the pang of jealousy. Norway was a fine country, and when he has taken Denmark from Sveyn he will have two kingdoms; but England would be a great prize. He would be as mighty as Cnut. And, from England, Norwegian sailors could journey further westward, discovering the new and wonderful lands he had heard about. He recalled the stories told to him by Brenn, of Lief Erikson and his father who had found a new world far from the shores of Norway. At the time he had imagined himself an explorer, a seaman, rather than a king. He turned back to Elisiv who was still reading her news:

- *Ann and Henry have their own battles it seems.*

- *Does he ask for help?* Harald looked to spread his influence.

- *No. It is not his battle he fights. He is playing a strategic game, something he learned from my father, I think.*

- *And what is this game of strategy?*

- *He has offered support to his young nephew, William of Normandy.*

- *The young bastard duke? Has he inherited the title?*

143

HARALD HARDRADA - THE LAST VIKING

- *There are rich barons circling, eager to take his title away.*
- *Such is the way for bastard sons.*

Elisiv drew a breath. It had been a constant source of worry for her, that Harald would take a woman, a concubine, to give him a son. But he would always be a bastard heir, so perhaps...

- *He has promised to help him hang on to his title as duke. They have beaten the rebels near Caen.*
- *So your father's dreams are realised. He has heirs in Hungary, in France, and perhaps one day in England, as well as here in Norway...*
- *And Denmark, too Harald.*

- *From here we shall be able to harry and chase Sveyn; raid the coast and wear him into submission.*
- *And,* Ulf reminded him, *we shall liberate the Viken people and bring them home to Norway.*

While Magnus had ruled both Denmark and Norway, there had been many meetings with the king to bring Viken back into Norwegian hands, but he had feared that the fragile peace he held would break, so he did nothing. Now Harald saw his chance to wrest back territory that sat on the Norwegian mainland.

- *My people will see that I have done what my nephew could not.*
- *Sveyn will resist...*
- *No-one will resist King Harald of Norway.*

Other messages had arrived. One of these occupied his mind. Finn Arnason had written. Harald owed him. His debt needed to be paid. Was it not Finn Arnason who had given him the power he had sought? Now was the time to repay the debt.

- *Come north to Austrått. You will be given a hero's welcome.*

HARALD HARDRADA - THE LAST VIKING

It was time to meet the earls at Giske. Finn had been like a father to him growing up in Ringerike. He owed him some filial duty as well as reward for helping Norway be rid of Magnus.

He went to Elisiv. She was resting in the shade of a newly planted orchard, hands resting on her growing belly.

- I have decided to journey north; to visit my kinsmen, and to hold court across the country.

- Am I to travel with you?

- You and Ingegerd will remain here, where it is warmer, and where you can bear our baby son.

- He kicks at me all the time now. Kicks like only a boy can.

Harald kissed her; and with Ulf alongside him, and a retinue of servants following behind, the King of Norway rode northward.

News of the king's arrival preceded him. Brenn and Dag were ready; the whole township was ready. Flags were flying above the cottages, and the raven standard flew high and proud above the moot hall. It was the first visit he had made to his home town since Magnus had died. They had all mourned the death of Magnus, but now they were excitedly waiting to see their new king; to see how the boy who had played in the fields of Ringerike had grown into his new role. They were all ready, but for Brenn and Dag this was a special day. Brenn knew that if he got his way, Dag would be leaving his home forever. They ducked through the doorway and took their places at the end of the table, near the doorway.

The king's closest family, his siblings were there. Guthorm and Halfdán, both rich farmers now provided much of the food that adorned the tables. They had forgotten the trials they had been

145

set by King Olaf, but Harald remembered. Here he was, his army feasting on the produce of his brothers' farms, just as he had said he would all those years ago. Gunnhild and Ingrid sat at the high table surrounded by their children, and horns blew marking the entrance of King Harald of Norway. The company stood and cheered as he came into the hall. The guards had been quartered in the town, but Ulf accompanied him, and took his place beside his king and friend.

Harald stood at the end of the table, the great carved throne, that was taken round the country from which he dispensed justice, waiting to receive him. But he stood awhile and looked round at the sea of faces. His kin, and his boyhood friends. At the bottom he saw Brenn and Dag, and he waved them forward.

- Come. You two shall have place of honour, for you Brenn made me the king I am today, and your son, Dag fought alongside me at Stikelstad, helping me to escape.

And he took Dag by the shoulder and embraced him. There were tears in Brenn's eyes, though later she would say it was the smoke from the firelight that had brought them.

- If you will give him into my charge, Brenn, I will take Dag with me, so that we can be warriors together again.

Brenn's heart was torn. She was proud that her son would be with his king; but she would miss him. Thinking of her own loss she said quietly to the King:

- Your mother should have lived to see this day.

- Ásta chose Magnus above me. Let's speak no more of my mother.

And the feasting went on long into the night.

When the king's retinue set off for Austrått, Dag rode alongside his king, alongside his boyhood playmate.

HARALD HARDRADA - THE LAST VIKING

Torah washed her hands. Again. Torah Torbergsdotter was nervous. In her dreams she had lived this day many times, but now that it was here, now that King Harald was coming to her door, she was afraid it would not be as she had imagined.

- What if he doesn't like what he sees?

Uncle Finn turned his wrist in a gesture to get her to turn round.

- Why would he not like my niece? You are very beautiful, Torah. Take it from an old man, he will see much in you that he likes.

- My face is plain, my hair the colour of straw...

- Even if that were the case, your hips are built to bear boys; to bear princes for Norway.

- And what about her, the Queen?

- You are the true Queen of Norway, niece. The word is she cannot bear him boys. They have a daughter, but now a second boy has died before its term. Harald is no fool. Tell her, Ragnhild.

Torah looked at her mother, looked to her for words of wisdom.

- Harald knows what he must do, Torah. He must live up to his promise, and you must do your best to persuade him.

- And if he doesn't want me?

- He will want you, her mother said, giving her a final look. *He will burn for you, Torah, as any man would.*

Finn turned her so that she faced him.

- And if he does not, then I shall remind King Harald, where his powers lie, where his interests lie. We are kin, by marriage, related to his brother, the sainted Olaf. Without our support, Harald will have difficulty hanging on to his power. He is not a king who is widely loved, as Magnus was and Olaf before him. He needs this marriage, Torah. He needs you. He needs us.

HARALD HARDRADA - THE LAST VIKING

They left her, and she sat on the high-backed chair that stood next to the bed. The room smelt sweet and aromatic. She, Torah, smelt aromatic. Oils and spices had been added to her bath, rubbed into her skin, and now she was ready. They had prepared her well.

- *What will the Queen say if you return with another wife; another Queen?*

Dag rode alongside his king, his boyhood friend. They had almost arrived. For some days now, he had seen the outriders, the spies who watched his progress towards Austrått. The Giske family made powerful friends, but deadly enemies.

- *Torah will not be my queen in the sense that Elisiv is. She will be my second wife. She is of good stock, where boys have grown strong. She will bear me boys and the country will be safe.*

- *And Elisiv?*

- *Will understand. Our daughter will become a queen, by marriage, by alliance; but a king needs sons if his line is to continue.*

Dag was trying to remember what she looked like, this Torah Torbergsdotter. He had seen her as a young girl, when she came with her uncle, Finn Arnason. Her remembered her wide smile, flaxen hair, long legs. He had to admit she was a beautiful girl. But not all beautiful girls become beautiful women. And even fewer become Queen of Norway.

- *She will be officially known as The King's Consort. And we shall have sons.*

- *So you intend to marry her?*

- *I intend to secure my Kingdom.*

HARALD HARDRADA - THE LAST VIKING

Dag stopped and looked at the town that lay ahead of them. They had been travelling South-West along the great fjord for some days, and he saw the houses perched alongside the sea. The blue waters were reddened in the setting sun. Dag hoped it wasn't a bad omen. He saw the small group of riders approaching. Harald held up his hand, and his soldiers stopped. They dismounted at his signal, and held their horses' heads. There was a silence as they watched the figures grow as they narrowed the gap between them. Dag stood in the silence and awaited their approach. He recognised Finn Arnason at the head.

It was late when the troop of men arrived. Torah had waited all day for Harald, and here at last he was. She felt unprepared for the sight of him, this huge man with his long yellow hair and his scars of battle. She felt a small trickle of sweat run between her breasts, as she watched him looking at her. She enjoyed the way his eyes studied her, drank her in.

- So, Torah Torbergsdotter. Here I am. As I promised.

- You were not a king when the promise was made, you were a prince then. And you did not have a queen. How is Elisiv? Has she recovered after... She stopped, unsure of what to say. *How is your daughter?*

- Well enough, both of them, when I set out.

Torah watched his face. She felt the tension in the air. She let him speak, in case her voice betrayed her emotions.

- The last time we met we sported together, Torah.

- Sported, your Highness?

- We played games in your father's pavilion. Board games. You beat me twice I think. But I was distracted.

- Distracted, Harald?

- Distracted by a beautiful girl with flaxen hair, wearing a long red dress.

HARALD HARDRADA - THE LAST VIKING

- She was a girl, Harald. Just a girl.

- A girl who tempted me and whose body pleased me.

- And does she still tempt and please you, King Harald?

- Yes. She does. They both stood still. Torah knew what he wanted.

- And are we to play more games?

- No more games, Torah. I have come to fulfil my promise, the promise I made to your kin and to you.

- And what will I be, when we are wed?

- You will be a King's Consort.

She smiled at him.

- And you will be Mother of Kings. Mother of Norway.

Night had fallen, and they made love in the shadows cast by the torches which sat in the sconces attached to the walls. And she remembered their first liaison, with its frisson and his soft caresses. But this was not like that. This was business. This was an affair of state. And her body ached from his weight upon her.

A week later, they were wed. In the traditional Norwegian way. The wedding, held as it should be on Frigga's Day, which dawned bright and blue. Harald had brought gifts with him: arm rings and finger rings were exchanged, and the feast prepared. Harald wore the sword given to him by his brother, Olaf, and Torah's hair was adorned in flowers. At last, she would have him. Harald was destined to be her husband as much as he was destined to be king. And although she could not wear the title Queen – yet – she would be at his side. Harald, Torah and Elisiv. It would not be the first time that a triumvirate had ruled.

HARALD HARDRADA - THE LAST VIKING

Dearest daughter.

Your family misses you. Kiev seems empty now that all of you girls have gone. Your father and I enjoy your letters. You are Queen and should never lose sight of that. Harald may have taken another woman but she will never replace you. You are his true wife. His Queen and your children will be rulers too. You carry on the great traditions of the Kiev Court. When you give Harald his heir, when you give him a son, this Torah Torbergsdotter will be nothing.

I understand how hard it is for you. But remember this does not diminish you. Harald loves you, and stands with you. In Norway you are Queen. He is building alliances that will keep you safe.

Elisiv let the letter drop into her lap. Her body still ached from the miscarriage, and her face still bore tracks of the tears she had shed. Of course she understood. Kings were not like other men, and they must do all they can to retain their power. But this was too hard.

When you meet her, be kind, be generous. Nothing will be gained by showing Harald you are jealous. Let her envy you. She wants what you have. And it might be good to have another woman in the court.

News of your new city is exciting. Ánslo sounds a strong name. Your father doesn't think it possible that it could rival our Kiev, but he is pleased that you use it as a pattern for this new home. Let me know when it is finished. And you tell me your palace is nearly complete. Perhaps, we shall visit, your father and me. We shall be the first guests in your new palace.

Elisiv longed to see her again. She missed her family, but especially her mother. And as Ingegerd grew she so resembled her mother it made her heart sore. And now they were on their way, Harald and his whore. All those years when Harald had

HARALD HARDRADA - THE LAST VIKING

rejected Magnus's claim to Norway because he was a bastard…
And now he plans to have bastard sons of his own. But perhaps
in the Norwegian way, if he has married this woman, her sons will
not be bastards. Is that what lies behind this? Her mother is right.
When they have a son of her own, then that woman can return
north, back to obscurity.

*Perhaps news of your sister and her Edward has reached you. His
claim to the throne of England has been challenged. He has gone
to Hungary to support Andrew in his fight for the kingdom there.
How good it is to have you, at least, settled and with a crown on
your head. You see, dearest daughter. There are always others
much worse off than yourself.*

She knew her mother was right. Of course she did. She should be
thankful to God for what she has. This other woman would not
take that away from her. She determined there and then to make
the best of it, until she had an heir for Norway. They were on their
way. Harald and Torah would arrive soon, a matter of days, she
understood. Now that she had a palace befitting her title, she
could welcome him home and show him how she had been the
"architect" of their new project.

There were still builders adding finishing touches to the outer
walls, but much of the building inside was complete. This was not
just some grand Moot Hall; it was a palace. She would show the
peasant consort what being royal really meant.

CONTESTS

Only God Himself decides
Which noble lord will win;
Fearless Harald of Norway?
Or Sveyn, the Danish King?
Which will steal the life and land?
Which will sink and tire?
The raven flies to battle, while
The dragon belches fire.

Dag watched him. His head was bent close with Thjodolf Arnarsson. Arnarsson and Harald had grown closer in the months following King Magnus's death. He remembered the skald from their days growing up in Ringerike. He had been a quiet boy, then, introverted, keeping himself to himself. He had spent his days with chisel and stone writing poetry. He had been good at it too; and it was no surprise that Magnus had sent for him to become court skald. Now, he was back with Harald, recording the deeds, following the journey into battle. Harald believed himself to be something of a skald, and Arnarsson wisely drew on his king's words - when advised.

The chase had been under way for many months. Sveyn, now self-proclaimed King of Denmark, had refused to yield the kingdom despite the constant harrying from Harald's ships. Denmark was difficult to defend, with so many islands, and Harald had swept through them but had never managed to catch up with Sveyn himself. He was elusive, and Harald was continually frustrated by Sveyn's ability to stay one step ahead, always one beat away. His Dragon-sailed ships continually thwarted the Raven sails of the Norwegian fleet. There were spies everywhere; we all knew that, and Sveyn was able to keep himself out of Harald's line of fire. The skald wrote every day of the *cowardly Sveyn*, who refused to engage, and his words were read in Denmark as well as in Norway. There were some in Denmark who would welcome peace with Norway, an end to the burning and looting, but they had no love for Harald. So they stayed loyal to Sveyn, biding their time. Magnus, the late King, had warned Harald that the Danes had no love for him, and would never support him as their king. All this Dag knew. He had the king's ear and Harald listened. But it was rare that Dag could change his friend's mind once Harald was resolved.

- Isn't it enough that you are King of Norway?

- Denmark is mine… and I shall not cede it to Sveyn.

- But he manages to stay clear of us.

- He is a coward; but we shall catch up with him, and we shall take the crown from his decapitated head. I myself shall do it. With my own axe.

It was time to change the subject. Dag knew his friend's moods.

- How is Torah? When is the child due?

Harald's mood lightened instantly.

- Any day now. It is a boy. My heir. And it is for the boy that I fight for Denmark. It his birthright.

- You know for certain.

Harald's hand went to his heart.

- I know in here. I feel it. And any day now, everyone shall know it.

News of Torah's pregnancy and the birth of the boy reached Elisiv in Ánslo. As she read the words, she held Ingegerd close to her.

HARALD HARDRADA - THE LAST VIKING

- You have a little brother.

- What is his name, mother?

- Your father has named him Magnus. And he shall be a king, unless...

- And will he and I marry, mother, so that I can be queen as you are?

- No, sweet child. Such a marriage is not allowed. But fear not, you shall be a queen. Your father and I shall make it happen.

- And will his mother now become queen?

- Torah is a king's consort. Mother of kings, perhaps, but I shall always be Queen.

And Elisiv remembered the promises her husband had made to her, his raven-haired queen. And, like him she was not content to be Queen of Norway, when there were so many other lands to conquer.

- And are they coming here, to our palace?

- They are on their way, Ingegerd. Torah and Magnus.

- Will I like her, mother?

- A princess, like a queen, cannot choose who to like. It is politic.

She spoke the words more to herself than her daughter. Elisiv saw the frown on her daughter's brow.

- Of course we shall like them. They will be our friends here in the court. And when he grows older little Magnus will be a playmate. Now go and get ready to greet them. Your green dress, I think, would be perfect.

Torah arrived without ceremony. It was her way. Her uncle, Finn Arnason, accompanied her, keeping the boy safe. Elisiv greeted her with formality, but with a smile and open arms too. Young Ingegerd hid behind her mother's skirts. Torah was clearly nervous, unsure of her place, despite all the assurances given by her uncle that she was as entitled as Queen Elisiv. But still she was fearful. The raven-haired Elisiv was as every bit as beautiful as the stories told.

- *How beautiful you are, my Queen.*

- *It seems my husband has had his head turned by your flaxen hair. My mother had your hair...*

- *And your daughter – our daughter – too.* Torah held her arms out, wide in front of her. The little princess looked at her mother, who nodded, and she crept into Torah's embrace.

- *I love you already, and I hope you will come to love me.*

Princess Ingegerd released herself from the embrace and moved back to her mother.

- *And where is Magnus? Can I play with him?*

- *He is asleep, now, Ingegerd. But when he wakes...*

This war of attrition was irksome to the king. Dag could see the impatience in every word, every gesture. When a man has fought so long and hard to become king, you would think he would take pleasure in it. But neither the king, nor his queen seemed satisfied. Messengers arrived from Denmark daily, and Dag was part of the inner circle, close to the king.

- *Sveyn becomes bolder. The man has the temerity to threaten raids. You see, Dag. You see why we must destroy him and reclaim the Danish throne.*

- *Is there not some way we can resolve this matter once and for all?*

Harald took him to one side, so that they would not be overheard.

- *Sveyn has challenged me to meet him at the Gota River in the summer. A fight to the finish. Or else, he suggests, we make a treaty, if I am too afraid to face him.*

HARALD HARDRADA - THE LAST VIKING

Dag felt the anger coursing through the King.

- I, Harald Hardrada, too afraid? No, Dag. We shall prepare for a final battle. We shall see who is afraid.

Dag had no doubt that Harald feared nothing. It would cost so many lives, but the king was determined. He saw it etched in the lines on his forehead, in the steps that he trod.

- Come, Dag. We must prepare for the mother of all battles.

Unseen by both Dag and the king, Elisiv had joined them.

- So at last we shall kill this cowardly Dane and take back what is promised to us.

Dag watched as the king and queen embraced. Together they would see all of the northern lands conquered and ruled, all the way to England. When he released her from his grip, she smiled and spoke to her husband:

- There is much to do Harald before we are Denmark. We will need more ships, more arms, more money.

Dag could sense the disaster that was likely to fall upon them. There were already mutterings - beyond the king's ear, but he, Dag, had heard them. Talk of disobedience was rife and Dag knew how his friend would respond. Norwegians were sick of war and strife. They remembered the days of Magnus as a Golden Age, and many wished he was still their king. But Harald and his queen were in no mood to listen to their complaints. They would listen to no counsel other than that of their own followers.

> **Norway's folk must by force obey;**
> **Declare their love for King and Queen.**
> **To stand and sit at his command,**
> **To show their utmost loyalty.**

HARALD HARDRADA - THE LAST VIKING

Dag tried again to count the ships, but could only have said there were more than fifty. They were lined up, laden with men and arms, ready for the final battle. They had sailed south. They would engage in a great sea battle. The Raven and the Dragon. They were at the Gota now, but news came that Sveyn held his fleet further south, off Zealand.

- See, he roared to his men, *even now, the cowardly Dane will not face us. He is afraid. He is a coward, but we shall harry him until we have his head on a pole.*

And his men roared and set sail again. As they chased Sveyn's ships, they set fire to towns and villages. Hedeby blazed; the men of Thyland fled, leaving behind women and children who suffered fates worse than death. All this Dag saw, and endured. His place beside his king, his boyhood friend, was secure so long as he worshipped at the altar. And then, at last, they came in sight of Sveyn's army. But the wind had turned, and a thick fog came down and obscured everything from sight. Dag hoped this might be an omen, that the king might see that it was not his destiny to fight Denmark. But in the morning when the fog cleared, the sight that greeted him froze his blood. He woke the king, who had drunk long into the night and slept through the dawn. They stood looking out across the sea, and many of the men had followed. They pointed at the sight.

- There are fires, Harald. On the sea, beyond us. The sea is on fire.

And Dag recalled stories of the Greek Fire that Harald had used in his days at Miklagard.

- Those are not fires. The Danish army is upon us.

- But the sea...

- That is not fire, it is the reflection of the sun on their gilded prows. Give the order to row.

HARALD HARDRADA - THE LAST VIKING

Dag called out to the men to go to their places and the message was passed through the fleet.

- Pull down the awnings. Take to the oars. The Danish fleet is upon us.

Sveyn had stolen a march on them. The Norwegian ships were slower and heavier laden. Water had spilt over the sides. Sveyn's ships were getting closer.

Queen Elisiv took her seat in the centre of the town square. This was her third court session, since her husband had been away. Ingegerd was back home, safe in the city with her stepmother. Elisiv hated to admit it, but she and Torah had become close in those days of fighting, when the man they shared was away in battle. She spent time with Torah and the children, and they were happy days in spite of the fears they had about Harald. She was a queen and must not be fearful. Her mother had taught her that. So many times, when her father had been away, fighting his enemies, it had been her mother who had kept her strong and dried her tears and showed her that duty comes before emotion. Torah showed her fears and concerns more readily. Elisiv saw the red eyes in the morning that gave away the tearful nights. But she kept herself from tears. They could serve no purpose, and meanwhile, the Kingdom must be governed. So here she was, in Trondelag. This was going to be a difficult morning. Einar stood in front of her. Just behind him and to one side was his son, Eindridi. He was a copy of his father, less broad, fewer grey hairs, but the same countenance. Neither had bothered with the usual courtesies, but stood, solid and square in front of her. She smiled

159

at the name by which the older man was known throughout the country.

- *So, Paunch-Shaker, what is it you desire from this court.*

- *I represent the farmers of Trondelag, Queen Elisiv.*

- *Surely, that is my husband's role. The King represents all Norwegian men and women.*

- *I am their leader. They have elected me to be their spokesman.*

Elisiv was wise enough to recognise what was brewing.

- *I'm sure they have little cause to need a spokesman, when here I am in the King's name, ready to listen to their worries.*

- *They need someone not afraid to speak his mind. Someone skilled in matters of law to represent them.*

Elisiv bit her tongue, and smiled at the man.

- *What troubles them, Einar?*

- *Your husband, the king is denying them their legal rights. He takes their lands and sells it to his friends so that he can raise more money for his war with Denmark.*

- *Their king is fighting to secure our lands, Einar. And as king he has the right to do as he wishes with the farms that lie in his kingdom.*

- *The law is mightier than the king. It is there to protect the lowest of his subjects as well as the king himself.*

- *The king makes the laws, Einar. Surely he knows what is right and what is wrong.*

- *It would seem not, my Queen. Your husband steals land from his own people. And theft is theft, whether it be committed by serf or by lord, by beggar or by king.*

- *Do you have a petition for me?*

- *I do.* And Einar Paunch-Shaker handed her the petition. *Here are men's names who have had land taken from them. I ask for them to be returned.*

HARALD HARDRADA - THE LAST VIKING

Elisiv made great show of looking at the list. She spoke with the three advisers who sat behind her, their heads close together. Then she turned back to this lawyer-farmer:

- *We have given due consideration, and we deny your claims.*

Einar opened his mouth but before he could speak, Elisiv waved him away. He stood still, refusing to move.

- *You are dismissed, Einar Paunch-Shaker.*

- *I will not be dismissed so easily. We northern farmers are a force to be reckoned with. And there will be a reckoning.*

Elisiv shivered. Had the clouds passed over the sun, or was it the force of this man that chilled her? This was no ordinary man.

The next petitioner was called forward and the proceedings continued. But she saw him from the corner of her eye, deep in discussion with a group of farmers. The morning passed and the Royal Court removed to a comfortable lodging for the night, preparing for the long slow ride back to the city. Einar Paunch-Shaker posed a threat. A threat that Harald would deal with.

RAVEN

- Sveyn was born in England. Did you know that, Dag?

Dag had heard the stories, but sorting fact and fiction was always a problem.

- I had heard that he was a nephew of Cnut. But born in England?

- Born there. And with a claim to that throne as great as mine.

- You think he means to rule England?

- Who knows how Sveyn thinks? But I must ensure that his ambitions are curbed.

Dag saw the whole game at last. This was not a battle for Denmark, but for a much richer prize. For England. They had escaped what had seemed a certain death on the "night of the fires". Harald had used every trick he could to flee the Dragon ships that night. The Danish fleet came on them fast and Harald ordered that the belongings of captured prisoners be jettisoned, assuming that Sveyn's ships would slow and gather them out of the water. But Sveyn ordered his ships on. At last, he had Norway in retreat and he would destroy Harald once and for all. The Danes rowed harder as they saw the Norwegians retreating. Harald then had all the ships' stores thrown overboard, partly to distract the chasing ships, mostly to lighten the load, to speed their flight. But when this failed to stop the Danes advancing, Harald ordered that all the Danish prisoners be thrown overboard. This time Sveyn could not resist. He halted his ships to rescue them. Some were pulled aboard, but most died there in the cold seas.

> **Dragon chases Raven,**
> **Into Jutland seas.**
> **Harald casts his prisoners,**
> **Watching as men freeze.**

HARALD HARDRADA - THE LAST VIKING

And so they escaped. Now they were returning home for reinforcements. The war would continue, until Sveyn or Harald lay dead; until either man's ambitions were achieved. This would be a long, drawn-out affair.

The city of Ánslo was in sight. Each time he returned, there was more to be seen. The city had grown. Queen Elisiv oversaw its building. And she had been busy while her husband had been away; busy making enemies, raising taxes to fund a war the people of Norway did not want. A feast had been prepared and the hall was full of laughter, of greeting and of the rich smell of cooked meats and vegetables.

From his place further down the table, alongside some of the king's most trusted warriors, he heard the raised voices. The hall was suddenly quiet.

- Einar threatened us?

Elisiv looked around at the silent hall:

- He keeps a force of men, and they follow him wherever he goes. It is a private army, Harald. He means to take power from us.

- That pot-bellied rebel shall learn what it means to threaten his king. He hopes to fill the throne with his fat arse.

A smile played on Elisiv's face. She remembered only too well her encounter with Paunch-Shaker.

- Even kings keep smaller courts than his, Harald. Einar, with his thrashing sword would drive us from Norway...

- Unless I first persuade him to kiss my axe.

The story of Einar's death was told to Dag by men who had been there, men who had killed him.

HARALD HARDRADA - THE LAST VIKING

Einar and his son Eindridi had been summoned to the court. He would be granted a royal audience and King Harald was in a mood to be generous. But just in case, the peasant army escorted him and awaited orders. In their hands they carried farm tools and axes.

- Wait here, with my boy. Wait for me to return. Stay armed, for I do not trust this King.

Einar entered the audience room. The torches had been extinguished and it was dark. Only the throne was visible, and the tall figure seated upon it.

- Why does the King sit in the dark?

But he got no reply. Figures rushed at him from the dark corners and hacked at him until he lay on the floor, a broken, bloodied heap. The noise of the attack had been heard outside and Eindridi drew his sword and rushed after his father in a vain attempt to aid him. His body lay where it was felled, next to his father's; both dead. The farmers outside the hall found themselves surrounded by the king's bodyguard, and though they urged each other to avenge their leader they were too afraid, and leaderless. It was the next morning, when she heard of her husband's murder, that Bergljot came to the farmer army calling on them to fight, to avenge their leader. They stood, ashamed of their weakness, and slowly the farmers broke up and left. Bergljot had the bodies of her husband and son taken to the tomb of King Magnus and they were buried nearby.

That was how Harald dealt with uprisings.

Sveyn was still raiding Norwegian territory and still avoiding the fight. Dag had led a number of expeditions chasing and harrying the Danish fleet. He sailed under the flag of the Raven, under the king's own banner, and he had some success, raiding and plundering, and returning home with riches - and prisoners. One of the prisoners, a woman who Dag judged to be around his own age, had been spared the fate so many of the other Danish women had suffered. Dag had arrived in time to keep her from the group rape that had been planned for her. He had taken her to his own tent, alongside the river. Now she stood before him, her torn clothes barely covering her body. Dag looked at her. It was sympathy he felt for her, much more than lust, but he felt that too. Here was the real victim of this vendetta. She and thousands like her.

- *Why does your King hate us Danes?*
- *It is one Dane in particular he hates? Your King, Sveyn. What a wretched king you have. He not only walks with a limp, but he's a coward as well. He will not meet our King Harald in battle.*

The woman looked at him

- *He is wretched yes, but he is not a coward. He has little luck.*

Dag laughed at her words, and gave her some clothes he had taken from the stores.

- *Wash yourself and take these. Dressed in these clothes you will look more like a Norwegian than a Dane and you will be spared.*
- *Spared for what?*

Dag knew what she meant. This was not the first time she had been threatened by invading troops, not the first time she had found herself naked with a Norwegian warrior. But it was the first time she had been given clothes to wear.

- *Am I to be spared to be yours?*
- *Would that be so bad?*
- *Do you know how to treat a woman?*
- *I know...*

HARALD HARDRADA - THE LAST VIKING

- Then I shall dress as a Norwegian, and live with my Norwegian warrior. My name is Stina...

- Stina? Has it a meaning?

- I am a Christian woman. Baptised. This is what it means.

- Stina. I am Dag Gaarder. And I shall treat you well.

She took the bundle of clothes from him and slipped out of the rent cloths she wore. She watched him as he watched her.

- Not too well, I hope.

And Dag smiled as he watched her move into the wash room. He picked up a jug of water and followed her. He had been lonely long enough. Svana had not survived the birth of his second child, and he had wept at her funeral. And in all that time he had remained loyal to her memory. But he was lonely, and this Danish woman would make a fine wife.

Finn Arnason was loyal to the King. He told everybody so. After all wasn't he Prince Magnus's great uncle? Hadn't he been like a father to the young Harald? And when the king came to Giske, he was welcomed. All the talk was of the death of Einar. There were many versions of the tale, but Harald gave them the "truth".

- If I had been there, I would have spared him.

- We heard you yourself had split his head with your axe.

- I would have spared him, Finn. I don't need rebel farmers marauding around the country. Some of my warriors took umbrage with Paunch-Shaker. They thought I wanted him dead.

- You are a hopeless scoundrel, Harald.

The king clasped the old man in a giant bear-hug.

- You know me well, Finn Arnason. As only a kinsman can. And as a kinsman I am going to send you to Nidaros.

HARALD HARDRADA - THE LAST VIKING

- That sounds like a punishment, Harald.

- I need the farmers to make peace with me. I want you to talk with them. They trust you.

Finn stood back from his king.

- And how will such a dangerous mission be rewarded? Those farmers from Trondelag hate you. They hold you personally responsible for the death of Einar and Eindridi. Anyone who goes to meet with them on your behalf will not be safe.

Harald took Finn's hand, and clasped it in his.

- You are the only man who can bring about a reconciliation. Tell me what you want in return.

- My brother, Kalf...

- He murdered Olaf. He murdered my brother...

- No, my lord. He was no more responsible for King Olaf's death than you were for Einar's... I want you to send for him. Bring him out of exile. Give him back his land, his titles, his authority, his revenues.

Harald took only a moment to consider it.

- Bring me the loyalty of the farmers and I shall bring Kalf back to Norway.

They shook hands on it.

At the feast that followed, talk was more familial; affairs of state were put aside.

- How is Torah? We miss her here.

- She thrives at court, Finn, as you knew she would.

- Thrives?

- She carries a second son.

- You know it is another boy?

- I feel it in my bones.

HARALD HARDRADA - THE LAST VIKING

Elisiv heard the screams. Her own son had been still-born, and she knew in her heart that she was never destined to give Harald an heir. Magnus would be King of Norway. And now, Torah Torbergsdotter was giving birth. To another son, she had no doubt. Elisiv's nails bit into the palm of her hands as she struggled to control her emotions. The whore brings two sons into the world while she has only a daughter. But she was queen. Torah would never take that title from her. Mother of Kings, yes, but never queen herself. Ingegerd ran to her, her hands over her ears.

- Tell her to stop, mama. Tell her to stop screaming.

- She will stop soon. It is what all women must do.

Her daughter looked at her. Surely not. Her mother and father would never let her feel such pain...

- And soon you shall have another brother.

- I think I'd rather have a sister, mama. Boys are so stupid.

- And what would you call her, this sister you want so much.

- Maria. Like the mother of God.

- I don't think any girl has been named Maria. Not in Norway. Back in Kiev, of course, I knew plenty of Marias...

- Then she shall be Queen Maria the First.

And Elisiv held her daughter close.

It was just after the screaming stopped, that young Prince Olaf was brought to her. She held the tiny boy; and envied the flaxen-haired Torah, thinking of her lost baby boy. Then Harald returned home.

HARALD HARDRADA - THE LAST VIKING

Since his banishment Kalf Arnason, had settled in the distant edge of the kingdom, on Orkney. He stayed with a cousin who owned land on the island and from there spent much of his time raiding the British Isles, with some success. When Finn sent word that he was to be allowed to return, and all would be restored to him, he made preparations to return home. Finn welcomed him home and, with his brother, he went to the king to be reconciled. Harald had returned to his battles with the Danes. They were sailing close to Fyn Island and word reached them that Sveyn had set a trap. As soon as they stepped onto the island they would be ambushed. It was while Harald contemplated his next move, that Kalf arrived on their ships, with a small troop of Viking warriors. More reinforcements for the battle. They met on the King's ship, where Kalf knelt before him, his sword laid in front of Harald's feet.

- *All the duties I showed, all the services I performed for King Magnus, I will now transfer to you, King Harald.*

And the King embraced him, like a long-lost brother.

- *I have a task for you, Kalf. One that I know you will be able to fulfil. Word of your adventures in Britain has reached us here, and now, we ask that you turn your skills to our fight with Denmark. And to show our love for you, I offer you the greatest victory of all. We shall launch our attack tonight on Fyn Island. Sveyn's troops do not expect us and you, Kalf, and these loyal followers you bring with you, shall bring Norway great victory and much plunder.*

- *We shall take great pleasure in carrying the Raven into battle.*

Dag watched them go, and said nothing. Harald knew where his enemies were, and there were as many at home as abroad. Finn and Kalf had arrived too late to hear news of the planned ambush. The trap was set.

The sun had not risen when Kalf launched his attack, hoping to catch the Danish force ill-prepared. But the battle did not last long. The Danish forces overwhelmed Kalf's warriors and their bodies were strewn across the fields. And at the centre, still holding his sword in his hand, lay Kalf. And that was how Dag found him, there on the battlefield. Harald had waited until the next day, then went ashore with the main force and when he saw Kalf's body, he stood and wept. Real tears, Dag noted. But the tears were for his dead brother. And as he stood over the body he mouthed:

- And so, my brother's murder is avenged.

He commanded that Kalf's body should be taken back to his brother, Finn, and that he be given fit burial for a Viking warrior. The Raven banner was carried further inland and they threw themselves onto the unsuspecting Danes, who had assumed the battle to be won.

> **A blood-stained sword was held aloft.**
> **Many Islanders lay dead.**
> **Fire consumed their houses**
> **As to safety others fled.**

Dag was not alone in suspecting the King of treachery, but he was not to be checked, not to be called to account. When they returned home, Dag asked for private audience. King Harald was in a good mood, and Dag felt it was the right time.

- You are my king and my friend. We have grown together, played together, fought together. But I would like to return home. I have taken a new wife...

- The Danish woman?

Dag smiled and nodded.

- ...and I want to show her off to my mother. She will be my children's new mother, and perhaps we shall have more children together.

HARALD HARDRADA - THE LAST VIKING

- *You knit our kingdoms more successfully than your King. Brenn will be proud of all that you... all that we have achieved.*
- *I think she will. I miss my home, and I am asking to return.*
- *To Ringerike? How I miss the old place, Dag. Its forests, its rivers...*
- *It is a land I want to grow old in, have more children and settle down. I know my mother would want to have grandchildren to cosset and guide, as she did us.*
- *There are few people a King can trust, Dag Gaarder, but a boyhood friend is one such. Give me one month more. Then you can return.*
- *Gladly, my King. I give it gladly.*

Later, when Dag and the woman lay together, he told her that he would take her home.

- *To meet your children?*
- *And my mother.*
- *And what will she make of me, your mother?*
- *She will love you as I do, and she will make you welcome.*

Finn Arnason was furious. He knew what had happened. This was yet another example of the king's true nature. He was treacherous and vindictive. What's more, he, Finn had been gullible, had believed the king when he offered forgiveness and restoration to his brother. What love there had been for the growing boy all those years ago, had now turned into hatred. Soon Harald would come for him. There were slights for which he would seek revenge, and Finn was not going to wait around for the midnight dagger. So Finn committed the ultimate betrayal. He went to talk with King Sveyn. In return for Finn's promise of

HARALD HARDRADA - THE LAST VIKING

allegiance, the Danish king appointed him Earl of Halland. He would be in charge of its defence against Harald's attacks.

HARALD HARDRADA - THE LAST VIKING

ENGLAND

Royal revenge left farms empty.
Royal revenge wore down the lands.
King Harald earned widespread renown
For the blood that stained his hands.

An uneasy peace was draped over Norway and Denmark. It was not a formalised pact; neither Harald nor Sveyn would ever have signed such an agreement. Scorched and blackened countryside, the bones of villages silhouetting the sky, large mounds full of the bodies of dead warriors: these were the monuments to the ceaseless battles, but both armies grew weary, and needed time to regroup and plan new strategies. Both kings knew there were still many battles to be fought, all in the name of vengeance and stubborn pride, but there was a lull, and Harald began to look elsewhere for glory. News of Harold Godwinson's visit to Normandy arrived in the city. Now established as a centre of trade and culture, the new city of Oslo, built on the wooden foundations of Ánslo, had drawn masons and carpenters from across the Viking world, and further east. Rus engineers and architects came at Queen Elisiv's request. And with those arrivals came news reports. Elisiv and Harald spoke together in the state room, its wide windows overlooking the harbour. Harald was restless.

- What is he planning?

- Godwinson?

- Aethelred. He has inherited the throne from his half-brother, but who will inherit from him?

- My sister's husband, Prince Edward still has claim.

- Edward will never be King of England...

HARALD HARDRADA - THE LAST VIKING

Elisiv looked at her husband and saw his ambitions burning in those bright blue eyes.

– And my sister will never be a queen?

- Not in England. Harald cupped her face in his hands, and kissed her on the lips, hard and long.

- That crown is made to fit your head.

And Elisiv ran her hands along his muscled body, and then returned his kiss, with an even greater passion.

- It is what I have dreamed of. But I hear Aethelred has already promised it to his foster-son. Godwinson. Perhaps our time has passed,, husband?

- And now Godwinson has gone to Normandy. I need to know why. I need eyes in their camp, someone I can trust.

- There are too few of those in the court.

- Not at court, no. But in Ringerike, there is such a man.

- You speak of Gaarder?

- Dag is one man I can trust. He has known me longer than any man. I shall send him to England.

- Will he leave his family so soon?

- Let them all go, together. It will attract less suspicion than a Viking travelling alone.

- Then send for him, my lord. Let him know how important England is to you...

- To us, my Queen.

Dag received the command with mixed emotions. He and the Danish woman had settled onto the farm at Ringerike, she had become his wife, taking Svana's place and the two boys would soon have a baby brother or sister with whom to share the crowded farmhouse. Stina had made a life here and now, with a new child coming, the timing was all wrong. She watched the two boys playing outside in the shallow waters of the fjord. These two boys had been strangers when she was brought to Ringerike. Now she thought of them as her own: Harald, named after Dag's boyhood friend and Erik, after his grandfather

- Take Harald. He is old enough now to accompany you. I am too far on with this baby of ours.

- We should be together as a family. Perhaps we shall find a new home in England.

- Husband, you have taken me from one home and I have done my best to make a new one here. And now that I am settled, now that your mother finally stops comparing me to Saint Svana, and she crossed herself in a mark of respect *– now that I am accepted, you want me to up sticks and move away?*

- You are my wife. Where else should you be but at my side.

- Your wife is also a mother, and she will soon be giving birth. How can such a hazardous journey be a good idea. Take Harald. He is a fine boy and he will learn much from the journey. He will see that there is life beyond Ringerike, as you did when you were his age.

Dag knew she was right, but he was disappointed all the same. She had become close to him, and Brenn had finally given their marriage her blessing. Stina and Dag were building a life for themselves, here on the farmstead at Ringerike. But she was right. The journey to England was not an easy one, and she was in no fit state to undertake the crossing. She needed to have Brenn with her when the baby came. He held her from behind, arms linked around her belly, and he smelt the sweet scent of her hair. And it wasn't just the journey that lay like a trap before him. He was to be a spy for King Harald, and if that became known...

HARALD HARDRADA - THE LAST VIKING

She sensed his concerns, felt him tense behind her. She eased herself so that she could look into his eyes.

- *Get ready, Dag. Tell Harald he is to accompany you on an adventure. You will go together to England.*

- *I hate to leave you, Stina. Especially now,* and his eyes moved down onto her belly, where he thought he saw signs of a kick.

- *Go! Do your king's bidding and then return home, to greet your new son...* she saw him smile, - *...for I am certain only a boy could kick his mother so hard.*

Within two days, Dag and his son Harald were ready, standing aboard a trading ship, bound for England. Stina had not come to see the ship depart. She had had a restless night and he left her asleep. Instead, it was Brenn who watched as the two of them climbed on board. She tried to hide her fears but he knew she worried.

- *Wave to your brother, Erik. He will be away until Spring.*

And young Erik waved his hand, tears on his cheeks. He would miss his father very much; he would miss his days on the floor of the forge, with his toy hammer, imitating his father's heavy strokes. And he would miss Harald too, though he would never tell him that. They watched as the ship's crew rowed into the middle of the fjord where the water was deeper; and watched as the sail was raised; and watched until the ship was out of sight, standing close to his grandmother, knowing that she too was crying.

Dag watched too, with tears of his own. He hated to leave but his king had a task for him and he would not let him down. They would sail first to Orkney where they would stop over for three days, trading and replenishing food and fresh water. Harald, his boy, had the look of Svana about him and he loved him for it. The boy spent time asking so many questions of the crew, and devouring their replies, each in turn raising more questions, until they sent him away. They landed in Orkney and he found a place to stay with an old family friend who had moved west some years ago. They spent the nights reminiscing of life in Ringerike, and Harald spent time with boys his own age. When they left, he could already see how much Harald had enjoyed this first part of the journey. He sent his first messages back home, and to the King before they set off again towards England.

The Orcadians – for such are the people of Orkney called – are true Vikings. Wherever I go they treat me as a long-lost cousin; they speak of you as their True King, and urge you to drive the Danes out from what are rightfully Norwegian lands. They are reluctant to return to Norway; they have made new and good lives here, but will provide safe haven for any assault you care to make on England, which is now ruled by the hated Anglo-Saxons.

From her dark corner of the State Room, Torah watched as King Harald turned to Elisiv, placing the letter to one side:

- *I told you he was a true friend.*

- *And it seems you made a wise decision. What else does he say of England?*

There is news that the Norman Duke William – he is everywhere known as The Bastard – is to make a journey to visit King Edward. They say he will be made heir, and perhaps it is true.

Once again Harald put the letter aside:

- *I suspected this. There are plans to hand England over to this Bastard. Despite the promise made to me that I would inherit it.*

Elisiv recalled the claim of her own brother-in-law young Prince Edward:

HARALD HARDRADA - THE LAST VIKING

- England is rightfully ours, Harald.

- England is a pawn; it is a gift made for any expediency. But it is our inheritance. This Confessor-King has no right to trade my birthright.

- What more does Dag say?

I shall journey westward tomorrow, and land where the Humber meets the Sea. There, so the Orcadians tell me, I shall be just as warmly greeted as they greeted me. In that part of England there are Vikings who believe the true King of England will come from Norway.

Torah listened to their talk, and to the news from Orkney. She failed to understand this king and his queen. Why could they not be satisfied with Norway? If she were queen, as she should rightfully be, Norway would be more than enough to keep her happy, and she would do all in her power to persuade Harald to stop this war with the Danes, and fix his eyes on this land, rather than England. But she was not queen, and she kept her own counsel. Her baby boy, Prince Olaf, reached for her breast, his lips puckering. She laid him to the teat and felt the flow of milk into his mouth.

It is a journey of several days, and I shall write when we land there. You are right, Harald, about the Viking nature. We are great explorers, and while the Danes and Swedes sail North and East, it is the great journey West that incites the Norwegian heart. I feel it, as I face the next stage of my journey. I hope your queens are well, and that Norway thrives, despite the constant raids from Sveyn's Danes. For myself, I am grateful for this opportunity to serve your Highness, as well as spending time with my boy, named for you.

Elisiv's brow puckered, and even at this distance, Torah could feel her blood rising.

HARALD HARDRADA - THE LAST VIKING

- Why does he say 'Queens'? Does this friend of yours not understand that Norway has only one queen, and that the other is a concubine?

Torah tried to bite her tongue but the words were out before she knew:

- A concubine who gives the king sons. A concubine who bears princes.

- I shall give my lord a son, and then your place at court...

Beside her, Harald slammed his hand down onto the table.

- Is it not enough that I have battles with Denmark? Will you bring more fighting into the Palace? Torah, leave us to talk. I shall come to you later.

Torah stood as tall as she could. In height she was Elisiv's superior, even if in status she were not. She tucked the shawl tighter round young Olaf and left the room.

- Am I to be reminded every day by that woman that I have not given you the gift you most want?

- You have given me gifts enough, Elisiv. Our daughter is as beautiful as any in the land, and she will make a fine queen in her time. Dag is clumsy with his words. You are Queen, you alone. But a queen must show magnanimity. A queen must reach out and make her peace.

Harald felt her bridle.

- A queen must do these things. Magnus and Olaf are my heirs and they will need their mother beside them as they grow. But they will also need a queen to show them what it is to rule. You must work together, you and Torah. For the good of Norway

Elisiv bowed her head in acquiescence. She knew in this he was adamant. She must learn to get along with Torah.

HARALD HARDRADA - THE LAST VIKING

- After all, my queen, she may one day be Queen Mother. When we have regained Denmark and when England welcomes me as king, you shall have other lands to rule.

He left her, following the concubine. She knew he would go to her now. But she did not mind. Since her miscarriage, her body was sore and she was not ready to try again for a prince of her own. She would make her peace. She would welcome Torah into her company. After all, should not the women work together to keep their husband's kingdom safe. And she smiled at his last words, mouthing silently:

- Elisiv, Queen of England.

Dearest Mother, how does my wife and son? My journey to Orkney has been pleasant enough, but I miss Ringerike. I miss those first steps and first words of Erik. I miss the warm bed next to Stina. Make sure she knows how much I miss her. And tell her too that her boy, Harald, becomes more a man every day. He grows strong and tall, and he is warm-hearted and generous. He is a fine son.

In Orkney there were many who knew my father, and your father too. Men who had worked alongside them in Ringerike's fields and who told me stories I had not heard before. The Orcadians love our king, and wait for him to be victorious over Denmark so that he can turn his eyes westward and rule over these islands. They talk of the mighty kingdom from Cnut's day: Norway, Denmark and England with all the isles between them. Only this time ruled by a Norwegian King with the blood of Sainted Olaf running through his veins.

HARALD HARDRADA - THE LAST VIKING

Tomorrow I shall sail to England. I have news that will not please the king but it will need to be checked. There is so much rumour and gossip here; it is necessary for me to see for myself and report truth to the king. The journey west brings to mind the adventures of Erik Thorvaldsen, that great explorer. Perhaps this is what I was made to be, a great explorer. Tell young Erik the stories of his namesake. Harald sends his love to all of you there at Ringerike.

They were right, the Orcadians. The Humber is an excellent place to land a force. The men here are true Viking soldiers; they only wait for the chance to overthrow their Saxon masters. It seems that conquest is the only way to claim your throne here. But be certain, you will be welcomed here, King Harald, with brave hearts and sharpened swords to fight by your side.

It is true. William has sailed to London. He meets The Confessor. Word is spreading that he has come to do a deal. King Edward has no heirs and William, as his close kin, seeks to be made successor. They say that the deal is done. I will journey southwards, along the coast to London. We have set ourselves up as a trader and many ships undertake that journey. In this way I shall keep eyes and ears open and report back to my king. My return to Norway cannot come soon enough, but I live to serve you and will stay a few months longer, returning before the winter storms.

Torah still felt uneasy. This 'new peace' that Elisiv had established in the palace left her uncertain. At least before she knew exactly where she stood. Now Elisiv's smiles and gentler speech made her wary. But she had to admit that her life was made simpler. The king divided his time between the two of them. All three children were together. They were a family – one with two wives and mothers - but that was not so unusual amongst kings and princes. And life *was* easier. Young Princes Magnus and Olaf were given the trappings that their titles earned and the younger prince especially was fussed over by their half-sister, Ingegerd, and by Queen Elisiv. It did seem that Harald's wish to bring them all together was being granted.

It was a cold rainy day and the boys were forced inside. They were keeping company with Ingegerd and the queen when she found them. As she entered the queen's chamber, she heard Elisiv talking with the boys.

- *... And together, you two boys, will rule over Norway, as Kings. And my son, for I am certain you shall have a baby brother soon, will succeed his father as King of England.*

It was all Torah had ever wanted.

1066

HARALD HARDRADA - THE LAST VIKING

JORVIK IS OURS. Harald returns to his ships. Victory is easy; too easy, I think. Harald himself will enter the gates tomorrow. Officials will be appointed and they will rule this great city in his name. The day is warm and fine. It is still summer here, leaves still green and flowers bright in the fields. We leave our armour on board. There will be no need for such protection against a fallen city. We are singing songs, and wielding swords and bows, thinking there will be little need to pierce bone today.

But it is too late. King Harold Godwinson has come in the night and locked the city gates against us, and behind them is a garrison of men. As we approach the town we see them. A large force of Saxon soldiers is riding towards us. Harald has sent for Tostig. Together they will wait and see what men these are riding against them and we stand watching as they grow closer and the force grows larger.

1063 - 1066

HARALD HARDRADA - THE LAST VIKING

GAMES

- I see your play, Torah. You mean to have my King.

The Tafel board was set out. Elisiv still called it "The King's Table", but she was still new to Norway. It was a game of strategy and women seldom played it, but she, Torah, had been taught as a child by Uncle Finn and had learned the strategies, the set moves, the best ways to protect the King-piece. But Elisiv was a quick learner. What she lacked in strategy was more than compensated by her ruthless approach. She would sacrifice pieces liberally, with no cares. And Torah wondered if she too would be sacrificed by this queen when the time came.

- How are you this morning, Elisiv?

She had stopped calling her "Queen", at Elisiv's request. They would never be equals but they were happier together now.

- The boy is ready to drop...

Elisiv pursed her lips, and studied the board.

- ... and I cannot wait to welcome him.

She moved the Bishop along its path.

- Perhaps he will kick less once he is out in the world.

- Boys love to kick, Elisiv.

It was in her nature to worry, and Torah was worried. What if Elisiv was right? What if her new baby was a son? Where would that leave her, and her boys, Harald's heirs? Torah suspected that Elisiv played life as she played Tafel, with a steely determination to win.

- This one certainly does.

Torah picked up Elisiv's king and laid it on its side.

- My game, Elisiv.

Torah felt her bristle. She hated to lose.

HARALD HARDRADA - THE LAST VIKING

- *This baby leaves my head in a spin, Torah. Let's put the board away. I shall play music instead.*

Torah watched as she waddled over to the large chest on which stood the stringed gudok, it's belly fat like its owner, and its strings as taut.

- *Perhaps the sound of music will draw him out, Torah.*

Torah watched as the Queen drew the bow across the strings. When she had moved into the palace, she had been struck by its foreign-ness. And this strange instrument was another example. It bore little resemblance to the lyre she herself played. But in the queen's hands it sounded just as sweet. Torah was mesmerised by the ebb and flow of the bow, as it danced along the strings. Suddenly the bow dropped with a noisy clatter. Elisiv's hand went to her mouth and Torah saw the pain in her eyes.

- *It's time. It's time.*

One of the women rushed to her, grabbing the gudok, before it fell to the stone floor. Torah took her hand and led her to the bedchamber.

- *Yes, Queen. It is time.*

Torah had not intended to stay. She didn't think that Elisiv would want her present at the birth, but the queen held her hand tight, squeezing hard.

- *Stay with me, Torah. With no mother to guide me, I hope you will stay. Please?*

And Torah felt pity for this woman. She may be Queen of Norway but she was a stranger, a long way from home.

- *Of course I shall stay. If that is what you wish.*
- *It is.*
- *Shall I fetch the King?*
- *When the boy is born.*

HARALD HARDRADA - THE LAST VIKING

When the child was born, Elisiv refused to come out of her room. Only Harald was allowed to see her. The new-born child screamed, as new-borns are wont to do. It was a week before Torah was asked to visit the queen.

- *We shall call her Maria.*

- *It is an unusual name for a Norwegian child. I know of no other.*

- *It is a perfect choice, for this girl of ours will be Princess of England, and they will welcome her with her Christian name.*

The birth of another girl was all the palace talked about. *The queen cannot bear boys; the king is being punished for taking a foreign bride.* And Torah found herself feeling sorrow for this queen. A son was what she had always wanted. And it seemed as if it was the one thing she could not have.

Harald made nothing of it.

- *Two beautiful daughters and two brave sons. What more could a man want?*

And Torah felt safe again. Her sons were her power.

But Harald was troubled. The problem that was Sveyn would not go away. Like a permanent itch on the skin, Sveyn could not just be scratched away. It was time to finish the Dane once and for all. But he would need all his resources for an assault on England. The Confessor King was aging. And there was a succession planned that would take the prize away.

It was not just Sveyn that irked him. Finn had been a spiteful enemy. Despite the ties of his youth, Harald could not persuade him to give up the raids that were more frequent than they had ever been. From his base at Halland, he was able to sail up the fjords and raid the villages in the south of Norway while the

HARALD HARDRADA - THE LAST VIKING

coastal cliffs and rocky slabs protected him from Norwegian raids. Harald sent messengers suing for peace but always the only reply was a single word: *Kalf.* His brother's betrayal and death drove Finn, spurred him. There must be another way to stop the raids. A final battle.

For his part Sveyn wanted to see an end to it all. The war between him and Harald, between Danes and Norwegians had lasted far too long. A decisive battle was needed. It would be better to lose than to face the constant harrying and skirmishing for another twenty years. He received the message from Harald, and sent one in return. Yes, he would meet him at the mouth of the Gota and there the war would end, one way or another. His fleet was almost ready. He had been preparing for such a day. Finn would lead them into battle. Nobody knew Harald and his tactics better. Sveyn knew how he was seen, both here in Denmark and in Norway: *the wounded bear* they called him, as much to do with his limp as his tall shaggy shape. His people loved him and knew he was a brave warrior but thought him an unlucky one too. *Courage alone doesn't win battles,* they said. Well, Harald and his Norwegian army would see what this wounded bear could do. They would taste his courage.

Finn had given him good advice.

- *To raise such an army, Harald would have to cripple his people with even more taxation. I know from my people in Austrått that they are already brought low by the cost of war. They will rebel, and he will have no army, no ships.*

So Sveyn prepared for war and hoped a depleted Norwegian army would come.

HARALD HARDRADA - THE LAST VIKING

The women of Nidaros stand and watch
As Norway's finest men pass by.
They watch as the oars rise and fall,
And wonder how many sons will die.

He sailed north while Harald's army of ships sailed south to meet them. When the storm came he pulled into shelter, but he knew that the Norwegians were caught in its power.

- God takes our part. He has a hand in this battle. He sends a storm to weaken the enemy. Remember that we fight with Him on our side. Even as I speak, the Norwegian army is cowering from us, hiding in the lee of the islands. How will he defeat us, if he cannot battle a storm?

When the storm eased, Harald continued south and arrived ahead of them at the designated battleground. Fleeing villagers reported to the Danish king that the Norwegian army was huge and waiting for them. Sveyn brought Finn to meet him.

- What should we do, Finn. You know this man. What does Harald expect us to do?

- He knows his numbers are greater. He knows this will be his victory. Wait. Tie up the ships off these islands and wait for him to grow impatient. He will not keep all these ships afloat, waiting, he cannot afford it. He will be forced to send some back. Then we shall attack.

Sveyn smiled at his new ally. He had proven himself since he had joined Denmark. Vengeance was a powerful whetstone.

It was a week later that the first reports came in. The second and third confirmed them.

- We have eyes watching Norway's every move. Harald cannot sneeze without my knowledge. He has set south again, but he has no more than one hundred and fifty ships. Less than half our number.

HARALD HARDRADA - THE LAST VIKING

Sveyn and Finn clasped hands, and Sveyn returned to his own ship. Finn stood at the bow of his huge vessel, as it cut through the water. He knew what he was planning would be seen as traitorous, but wasn't this king a traitor to his people? Wasn't he a villain who must be crushed?

- We have reports, my lord, that Sveyn's fleet is twice the size of ours. Over three hundred ships are sailing north to meet us.
- Three hundred. Good. Then more Danes than Norwegians will die today. Harald stood balanced evenly on the deck of his great serpent-ship. It was a council of war. Alongside him Ulf Ospaksson looked around at the men aboard Harald's ship; their mood was the same as his own men.
- They are afraid. These are brave men, but they fear they will die before this day is done.
- What would they have me do? Run from Sveyn?
- Regroup. Return with a bigger force.
- I would sooner lie dead, surrounded by these brave men than flee from battle. This is my Stikelstad, my battle but this time Norway will be victorious.
Ulf returned to his ship, relaying the King's message. Watching him return on the small rowing boat, Harald called his skald to him and spoke softly so that he could not be overheard.
– You will have much to record, before nightfall. I know these men are afraid, but they are brave too.
Thjodolf Arnasson looked out to sea, watched the waves rise and fall, lifting first bow and then stern, and words began to form in his head. **A tryst to please the ravens... feeding corpses to the wolves...** Harald left him standing, lost in his own poetry.

HARALD HARDRADA - THE LAST VIKING

That night the warriors camped on the edge of the fjord. He called them together, ordered them to fill their tankards, and stood head and shoulders above them:

- *Be steadfast and be ready. Make a bulwark of shields. Line our longships so tight that no gap can be found to pierce our wall. And behind this rampart, have your spears and axes and swords ready.*

Alongside stood Ulf, his sword raised in defiance. He added his battlecry:

- *Let us row into battle. Let us defeat these Danish farmers, and all of you who are here will have their names written into history.*

Sveyn clapped his hands. Harald was here. And victory was assured. He had done well in listening to Finn. He had brought them here. Now his luck would change and his poets would write about his victory and his name would be revered forever. They had reached the mouth of the Nissa river, so wide that it was difficult to see detail on the banks that rose on either side. The mist was only just clearing and ahead he saw the Norwegian ships waiting for him. He lowered his hand in signal, as the first arrows rained down. The ships grew closer and the men swung grappling hooks.

- *Let battle rage!*

> **Shunning shield and armour,**
> **Great warriors, both stand.**
> **Locked in bloody battle,**
> **Fighting hand-to-hand.**
> **Rocks and missiles crushing down,**
> **Swords stained red with blood.**
> **Arrows raining down upon**
> **Their heads, till few men stood.**

HARALD HARDRADA - THE LAST VIKING

The baby girl lay resting in Elisiv's arms. At last she slept. She had spent the night restless and screaming. Torah had taken turns with her, rocking the baby back to sleep. But only this morning had she settled, and now Elisiv, having been awake all night, dozed with baby Maria. Torah watched them. The scene was disturbed by the sounds of heavy boots.

- *Do you bring news of the battle? How is the King?*
- *King Sveyn's banner has fallen. Denmark is defeated.* The sound of voices woke Elisiv, though Maria still slept. She took in the scene quickly:
- *And the King?*
- *The King is well. He fought with courage and bravery. He is already making his way home.*
- *He is not hurt?*
- *An arrow pierced his coat, but he broke it off and fought on. He bled a little but his is well. When the king was struck he fell back, but it was Earl Hakon who sealed the victory. He rowed against the Danish fleet who were trying to encircle us when they saw the king fall. But Hakon drove them back, until the king stood tall again.*

Elisiv looked at her child. Maria sucked her thumb, a look of calm and contentment overwhelmed her.

- *I think she knew. She knew the peril her father faced. Hakon will be rewarded. He is a brave warrior.*
- *He is, Queen Elisiv, but none was braver than the king himself.*
- *And Sveyn?* It was Torah who asked the question. – *What of the "wounded bear". Is he dead?*
- *No, Lady Torah. He escaped.*

HARALD HARDRADA - THE LAST VIKING

- You mean he jumped ship leaving his men to die?

- Yes, my Lady.

- And what of Finn Arnason? He was still her uncle and, even now, she hoped for a reconciliation with Harald. *– What of him?*

- Taken prisoner. He is returning with the King, in chains.

- We meet again, Finn Arnason. You have returned to court.

Elisiv watched the old man, hands and neck bound, his feet still chained. His head moved as he tried to see clearly.

- You have learned what it is to be a traitor, to your country and your King. Your new friends, these Danes have not stood beside you.

- I have learned what it is to grow old among friends, even in a foreign country.

- My husband has shown you mercy and spared your life. He is merciful. He gave orders, I believe, to keep you alive. He gave them the unpleasant task to drag your old blind body home.

- Norwegians are given many bad orders these days.

- Do you want your life spared? He has given you to my charge, and it is I who will decide if you live or die. Do you want to be spared?

Finn did his best to stand tall but the ropes that bound him held his head in a stoop.

- Not by your husband. He is a dog!

- Perhaps you should ask your kinsman, young Prince Magnus, for his mercy? He was in the battle, in charge of one of the king's ships, where you would have killed him.

- That puppy?

HARALD HARDRADA - THE LAST VIKING

Through the milky mist that clouded his eyes he saw another figure approach him. He recognised her voice when she spoke.

- *Will you then accept your life from me?*

- *Are you here, Torah?*

- *I am here, Uncle.*

The old man stood, stooped. His eyes filled and the tears ran down his face. His hands were bound so he could not wipe them away. But he said nothing. Elisiv stood in front of him and pushed his shoulders down so that he landed on his knees. When he tried to stand, the guards who stood either side held him down. In that position he listened to the queen's judgement.

- *You may return to Sveyn. In respect of your age, and the memories of his youth, and your kinship to Torah and his sons, your king has given you leave to go back to Denmark. You will be returned to Halland.*

The old man was lifted up onto his feet and dragged backward to the door which closed behind him. King Harald stepped out of the shadows. Torah thought she saw signs of tears on his face. Though perhaps they were her own that confused her.

- *Is he gone?* Torah nodded, then she followed her uncle out of the room.

- *Done like a true queen, Elisiv. Like a true queen. I have dismissed all the warriors. They have returned home so that they can share with their families the brave deeds they performed. Earl Hakon has been lauded high and low.*

Elisiv smiled and took his hand.

- *The soldiers will name their sons after him.*

- *Some of those soldiers have brought me different news of this brave earl. It seems he is not above a few games himself. It is not just Finn Arnason who betrays us. It seems he allowed Sveyn to* escape. I am thwarted at every turn, to bring the Kingdoms of Norway and Denmark back together.

- What will you do, love?

- I have already sent soldiers to his house. It seems someone warned him we were coming for him.

- He escaped?

- To Sweden, where King Steinkel has made him provincial lord at Varmland.

- Will you send for him?

- Let him rot there. I am tired of his games. And I am tired too of all this trouble with Sveyn. I have had the scribes draw up a Peace Treaty. Sveyn will sign it. I shall relinquish my claim on Denmark. You and I, Elisiv, can now prepare for a different battle.

- For England, Harald?

- For England.

HARALD HARDRADA - THE LAST VIKING

CONFESSOR

- They are a nest of vipers. They plot and plan a succession which has no place for you, Harald. They thwarted my sister and her husband's legitimate claims, and now they thwart us.

Word had come from England. The contacts Dag had established had turned into a network of spies. Nothing happened in England that was not reported back to Norway.

- There are men – good fighting men – waiting for you, Harald. Men who will fight by your side when we invade.

Harald said nothing. He stroked his chin, a habit that made him seem wise but one that he used now to give him pause to think. He was less reckless now, more prone to bouts of seeming inactivity, when he used the space between actions to scheme. Success in England would not come from rash moves.

- We are not yet ready, Elisiv. Our forces are weakened from the years of struggle against Sveyn. In any case, Ethelred's son still lives and sits upon a throne. He is known across the land as Edward the Good, whereas...

Elisiv put Maria into the child's chair, a miniature version of her own queen's throne, and moved to her husband. She took both his hands in hers and felt the strength of them.

- Whereas you are known as Hardrada, which in their language they translate as ruthless, savage...

- They will not go up against Edward, even the Norse-born. They love their king. He is tolerant, gives them freedoms. He is a man of God. Though he is Ethelred's son, he is not like his father. You know what they said of his father? That he was 'unready', that he was unwise and made a poor king. It was his rule that gave the Saxons more power and weakened the Viking territories. They despised him. But Edward is different.

197

HARALD HARDRADA - THE LAST VIKING

- So what shall we do, then? Give up our rightful claim?

Harald looked her in the eyes and saw there the steely determination; he had fallen in love with her face, those eyes, that steel, and he loved her still for them. She was a woman fit to be queen.

- No, Elisiv. We shall wait. He is an old man, into his sixties now, and he has no heir, none except Harold Godwinson who he has adopted as a foster-son. Godwinson is Earl of Wessex, whose power has grown under this King. The Vikings have no love for the Wessex men. They will not take kindly to his inheriting the throne.

- But King Edward's wife is a Norman and she will speak for the bastard Duke William.

Harald smiled at her, and held her close. He felt her heart beating against his chest.

- And in this confusion, I shall take what was promised me by Magnus and great Cnut's son. We must be patient, Elisiv.

The queen moved out of his caress but held both his hands in hers.

- And when did my husband learn to be patient? When did he stop being the bull at the gate?

- It is something my brother taught me. 'There is more than one way to win a battle'. We spoke together on the eve of Stikelstad.

- A battle he lost, Harald...

- A battle where he was betrayed. I think he knew that he would die there. He knew he had been betrayed. I will not make the same mistake. England will be ready for the plucking, and I must prepare myself for the time that will come.

He left her there, in the bedroom. She watched him go, and turned again to her daughter, lifting her out of the 'throne'.

- So, Maria, your father has become a philosopher. I hope he is not going soft, that he will settle for Norway. England is the prize. England is our destiny.

HARALD HARDRADA - THE LAST VIKING

The journey to Ringerike was easier now. There were well-ridden routes. Harald's journey was taken in secret, for it was not safe for this king in every corner of his kingdom. It was in Dag Gaarder's farmhouse that he stayed. And when he left the next morning he rode alongside his boyhood friend.

- *Is there really no-one else you can send, Harald? In all that fine city of yours?*

- *'The finer the city the fouler the people' – surely you know the adage, Gaarder.*

- *I certainly wouldn't swap its walls for my own farmhouse. And must I go to England again?*

- *There is no-one else I trust. Our people there know you. They know you speak for me. And I know you too. I know you will speak the truth on your return. I know you will miss your family, but they will be here when you return.*

- *But will my mother still be here?*

Harald recalled their brief meeting last night. She seemed frail, this nurse of his; the confidante of his youth, was an old woman. She had lived beyond her span.

- *Brenn will wait for your return. Like she has always done. She will not die while her son is away. And your wife and children will run the farm in your absence. And I promise you, this will be your last visit to England...*

Dag smiled, and spurred his horse on so that he left Harald behind. Harald would always come to him for these 'special' tasks. He was valuable to the king, and he had benefited from their relationship. He heard the king pull alongside him.

- *Unless of course you return to have me crowned there.*

HARALD HARDRADA - THE LAST VIKING

Dag knew what he had to do. He would join a trading-ship again and once in England he would meet with old friends from his last visit. There was one man Harald had identified in reports, that would be useful to him. He remembered the conversation which had gone long into the night.

- Tostig Godwinson, Harold's brother, but not a loyal kinsman. He rules in Northumbria against the people's will. He has been in conflict with his brother Harold for some years. He has an army and he plans an attack on Jorvik. He has friends in Flanders and can provide a diversionary attack, when the time comes, in the south of England. He will prove a useful ally. Let him know he will be well-positioned in the England under Harald Hardrada. Few men can resist power.

Harald shared with Dag all the knowledge he had on Tostig. And Dag had the seeds of a plan as to how to arrange a meeting. Jorvik was the way in. There were men enough who hated the Saxon powers that had conquered and held Jorvik in the Saxon King's name. These were Harald's natural allies, and they would join Tostig against the city. There was also news of Harold, Tostig's brother. He had been shipwrecked along the coast of Normandy and the rumour was that he was being held by Duke William.

- Find out all you can. The time is coming, Dag, I feel it in my bones. And Norway must be ready – I must be ready – to take what is promised me.

When they parted company close to Oslo, Dag joined a merchant fleet bound for England.

Harold Godwinson was brought in chains to Duke William's fortress in Rouen.

HARALD HARDRADA - THE LAST VIKING

- I have rescued you from the clutches of Guy de Ponthieu.

The duke's speech was heavily accented but Norman was one of the languages of the English court so Harold needed no translator.

- Duke William is a noble ruler, a man of honour. England will not forget his kindness.

William looked at his captive. He was a tall man, with the fair hair worn long, typical of the Saxons. William let the silence hang in the air, then when the thoughts were carefully aligned he said:

- And how does my cousin, Edward? I hear his health is...

- My sister's brother is well, and will live for many years.

William smiled, Harold was playing his hand well, trumping his own connections with the Confessor. But he doubted his spies were wrong. The time was coming when a new king would be crowned, and why not him, William. He was safe now in his own realm. Few dared challenge his claim, bastard though he was. The rebels who would take Normandy from him were crushed. Now was a time to look across the sleeve of water that separated him from his true destiny. One that had been promised him. His thoughts were interrupted.

- Am I your prisoner, Duke William?

There was a long silence as William let the thoughts come before he spoke.

- Unchain him. Make this Saxon Earl welcome in the court. And when you are refreshed, Godwinson, return to me so that we may talk about your safe return to England.

When Harold returned it was dark, and the tables were laid out for the feast.

- This is in your honour, Harold. We treat our English cousins well.

Harold waited. He knew there was more to come. But the duke would not be hurried. He was a man who thought about his words, and made no rash statements. The meat was already on his plate when the duke resumed.

- I would prefer it if you stayed at court awhile, here in Rouen. You will be treated well, in line with your position as Earl of Wessex, and family of the King of England. There is much for us to discuss.

- The weather is conspiring with you, Duke William, and persuades me to stay.

The feast continued and the duke turned to his nobles, and left Harold to himself. Harold knew what William wanted. And he knew that if he was to return home – alive that is – then he must give this Duke of Normandy what he requested. Norman food was rich and savoury, so a few months spent in this realm would do him no harm.

It was some time later that Harold was summoned to the duke. Until then he had spent much of his time talking with the duchess, Matilda. She had her own plans it seemed.

- Tell me Harold, what is it that you and the duchess talk about?

Matilda sat coyly behind her husband, her hands in her lap. There was a small smile on her face.

- We have been plotting behind your back, my lord.

Harold watched the effects of his words. But William gave no sign of concern.

- So it would seem, Wessex. And what plots do the two of you hatch?

- The Duchess, your noble wife has been matchmaking.

William turned his shoulder towards Matilda, and Harold saw the smile grow between them.

- My daughter is very young to be wed, Harold.

- I have agreed to our betrothal. And I shall return in five years for her hand... if you are in agreement with your wife.

HARALD HARDRADA - THE LAST VIKING

- We have talked about this, Harold. There are no secrets between us. It will be a good match: for Normandy, for England, for Wessex, and for Adeliza herself.

Harold smiled. It was an easy matter to make a betrothal here, under duress, and to break a promise back on safer shores.

- She is a girl with much beauty... and she is truly devout.

- She is her mother's image, Wessex, and she will grow even more fair.

- Then I shall be blessed by such a union.

Silence fell about them again, and Harold knew William was preparing his next gambit.

- And as my son-in-law you would have no reason to oppose my claim to the throne of England.

So here it was, as Harold had known it would be. This was the real matter, the crux. But Harold doubted that The Confessor would live long enough to bless the union.

- On what, Duke William, is such a claim based?

- It was promised me. King Edward himself sent his Holy Archbishop to give the news, to make me his heir.

- And you fear the promise may be forgotten, William?

- I fear that, though he is a good man, Edward may not be able to resist the temptation to give his throne to a Saxon Earl.

Harold knew his place. He knew his safety depended on his reply. What he said was:

- If what you say is true, then be in no doubt, as your son-in-law, I should not oppose such succession. Indeed, I would welcome you, William, with open arms. You have my solemn word.

What he thought was somewhat different. Back in England, where his base was strong, where his own succession was guaranteed, such an oath, made once more under duress, would count for nothing.

HARALD HARDRADA - THE LAST VIKING

On Dag Gaarder's return to Oslo, King Harald summoned him to the court.

- Your suspicions are well founded, my lord.

- So William and Harold plot the succession between them.

- From the news I gathered, both have claims to the throne and although Godwinson has given his oath to support the Bastard, no-one really believes he will give up his own claim. They are both preparing for war when King Edward is dead.

Harald sat, stroking his beard.

- And what of Tostig? What of Norway's allies?

- That is still brewing. Harold's brother has a tenuous hold over his lands, and Jorvik is in rebellion. They are raising an army to throw him out. But they are still too weak. It will be spring before they have the strength of arms.

- How does that suit Norway? Surely we shall need Tostig. We shall need Jorvik on our side.

- If Jorvik falls to rebel rule there will be war there too. Tostig will be banished, and he will bring his army with him. Tostig and Harold, already at odds, will be sworn enemies before another year has passed. He has eyes on the throne himself but would not oppose your claim, if he can see advantage to himself. He is a strong ally, and will bring a ready-made army to join your troops. They see you as successor to Cnut, and will fight by your side to bring back those good old days.

Elisiv smiled. She sensed the time was coming for her to do what her sister had not managed, to become Queen of England. It was her question that got to the heart of things.

HARALD HARDRADA - THE LAST VIKING

- And what of Edward himself? Is he as hale and hearty as some would have us believe?

Dag turned to her, saw the light burning in her eyes.

- There are rumours a-plenty, my Queen. I have heard from someone close to the King that he has dreamt of his own death.

- And what was in this dream?

- My lady, it is fanciful nonsense.

- Nevertheless, I am certain we should be grateful for its being shared.

- I was told that Edward dreamt that within a year of his death, God would punish the whole of England by delivering it into the hands of the enemy, and 'devils' shall come through the whole land with fire and sword and the havoc of war...' While we cannot trust such things, a man who dreams of his own death, may be nearer to God than others tell.

Elisiv held up her hands to silence the messenger. She moved towards her husband and took the King's hands in her own.

- God has sent his pious saint a message, and Hardrada will deliver God's word.

Dag's journey home was a slow progression. Winter storms felled the trees and blocked his route. When he eventually arrived home, the farm was empty. He made his way to his mother's house; there everybody assembled. Not just his family, but members of every family in Ringerike. And there were tears. Brenn was lying in her bed, an old woman now, aged rapidly in those months he had been on his errand. He cursed the king silently for taking him away from her; but Harald was right. Brenn had waited for his return. She pushed herself higher in the bed and held out her hands to him. There were no words; she was too weak for words, but her eyes spoke. In them he saw the love she had held for him, the devotion, and he held her outstretched hands and felt her strength die. Brenn was dead. She had waited for her son to return, waited so that he was the last thing she would see.

The funeral was held on the second day. She lay in the cold ground covered in a linen sheet surrounded by the tools she had used all her life, her spoons and knives, her loom. And as the earth covered her, Dag stood, holding his Danish wife and their three sons, his arms wrapped around them. Stina's face was wet with tears. Brenn had been a good mother to her, kind and warm. And her grief was real.

- The king should be told. He loved this woman. And she loved him.

And Dag held her close. Word would be sent, but he would not leave Ringerike again.

HARALD HARDRADA - THE LAST VIKING

SUCCESSION

Norway: warrior, king
Turns eyes unto the West.
England's burial plots
Will be filled with Norway's best.
Carrion crows will follow
To feed on soldiers, brave.
They know that battle will provide
As men fill up their graves.

The Gods were plotting and he, Harald Hardrada, knew that he had a major part in these plots. Elisiv saw England as the prize. It was the Kingdom her heart was set on. But for Harald it was another stepping-stone. If he was to be immortal; if he was to become, as he believed, the greatest Norwegian of them all, then it was the lands beyond he would conquer, those that lay far across the sea to the west. Vinland! England was merely a stepping stone to his ambition. War was coming and his forces were almost ready.

Nothing, he knew, was more dangerous than a brother who thought his birthright was stolen. It went back to Jacob and Esau, those brothers in the bible, that he'd read about as a child. Look what that had led to... Perhaps it was Tostig who held the key. News had arrived this very day, that Tostig Godwinson had been spotted off the coast of Denmark, with many ships in support of him. He was Sveyn's cousin, and Harald feared that the enmity that had long existed between himself and the Danish King would not help his cause. But Sveyn was in no position to help Tostig win England. Harald decided that he would use some of the hidden supporters he had embedded in Sveyn's court to make sure that Tostig knew where his true friends were – here in Norway.

HARALD HARDRADA - THE LAST VIKING

Elisiv watched her husband as he stood, staring out of the window, and she knew his thoughts.

- *Send for Tostig, Harald. Let him know his best hope lies with you. Sveyn barely has the strength to hold Denmark. He has no stomach for a fight. He has no ambition.*

- *Sometimes, Elisiv, I think I have too much ambition. When a man has fought so hard to capture a kingdom and to rule it, why should he not be satisfied then?*

- *But you are no ordinary man, Harald.*

She moved behind him, her eyes looking out to the westward horizon where his were focused. And her arms wound round him, her hands clasped together at his chest. She knew he could feel the warmth of her through their clothes. She knew he still desired her, and she knew his desire would spur him on.

- *You are no ordinary king. You are Harald Sigurdsson, born to be King of Norway and of England.*

- *And of Vinland.*

- *And of Vinland too, once we have the first prize.*

- *And how would we gain such riches, Elisiv?*

- *Your sons will rule here in Norway. It will give Torah great pleasure to see her – your – sons rule here. Then our future sons will rule England and you will sail west in the wake of the Great Erikson and become even more famous than him.* Elisiv knew where his ambitions lay.

- *But before that, we must take England.*

- *I will send for Tostig Godwinson. I will ask him to join us against his brother, when the time comes, and in return, I shall give him great powers in the land he covets.*

He felt her squeeze him, and felt his blood run hot as he felt her contours against him. He turned, held her high and took her back to bed.

HARALD HARDRADA - THE LAST VIKING

Harald's message had been well-received, and Tostig turned his fleet to Norway.

King Edward was dying. Harold Godwinson and all the Earls of Wessex stood by the bedside. The Saxon chewed his lip. This is just what he'd feared. The old man had still not put the seal in his hand, the ring on his finger. How many other claimants would appear when the Confessor took his last breath? He watched the rise and fall of the King's chest, slow, weak. There was no doubt he was dying and Harold must act fast if he was to take what was rightfully his. The year's end had passed and the new year had come, cold and dark. Harold had to be sure that darkness and chaos would not follow. He knew he had the support of most of the Witan. These "wise men" – how appropriate a time it was for them – were the king's closest counsellors. And more than anything else they sought stability. England was a more peaceful settled place now. They did not want war and unrest to follow. Harold knew they saw him as the strongest, safest option of all the claimants. When a king dies without issue, it leads to dangerous times. Yes, the Witan would support him. But they might need his intervention. A plan formed in his mind:

- *The King sleeps. Let us leave him to his dreams and return in the morning. I shall stand vigil and send for you if he wakes.*

He could sense their reluctance to leave their king at this moment. But he ushered them out of the chamber, took out his great sword, and stood holding it with the blade balanced on the floor.

- *No-one shall pass but through my sword. He is safe this night. Leave one of the boys, the king's servants by my side. He will bear witness to my actions. I shall send him if he wakes.*

HARALD HARDRADA - THE LAST VIKING

The bedroom emptied slowly. Old men shuffled out into the crisp cold night. The hallways and corridors still bore the remains of the Christmas Festival. Under the Confessor it was a time of more fasting than feasting, and felt very distant from the old Yule celebrations that Harold had heard about, and were still practised in parts of the country. He, Harold, once he was King of England would put a stop to such paganism. The old Viking ways would become a thing of the past. He signalled to the valet to close the door fast behind the retreating backs, and he called him over.

- Stand and watch with me, boy. Give your king due reverence. Keep awake, and watch with me.

And together they stood, heads bowed, as the old king slept. Harold knew he would never awaken from this sleep, but he must turn this to his advantage. From the corner of his eyes, he watched as the young man's head slowly drooped. He took up a place next to Edward's bed and leaned his ear to the king's mouth. The breath was stale and weak. He reeked of the afterlife already.

- I hear you my king, and your word will be my command. You may trust both your widow and your kingdom into my protection.

Harold spoke loudly enough to waken the groom.

- So you are witness to his words!

The boy looked confused, still emerging from his sleepy state.

- My lord?

- You heard him speak... just then... into my ear.

-My lord? Harold saw the confusion in his eyes, and his hand gripped tighter on the sword.

- You were awake, were you not?

- Yes my Lord. I was awake. I am awake.

- Then you must have heard his last words.

- His last words, my lord?

HARALD HARDRADA - THE LAST VIKING

- *Commending to my protection his widow and his title, his country. You must have heard that if you were awake.*

- *Yes my lord. I heard the king speak.*

- *Our friend and king is dead. You must go to the Witan, who will have reassembled, I am sure, in the Great Hall. Tell them what you saw, what you heard.* Harold saw the confusion in the boy's face. And he also saw the sword in the Earl's hand.

- *I will, Earl Harold. I will go straight away and tell the Witan it was as you have said.*

- *No, boy. You will tell them it was as you heard! Or will you tell them you fell asleep on this night?*

- *I will tell them what I heard, my lord. I will tell them.*

And the boy scrambled away, down the long, shadowy corridors to report that the King and the Kingdom had passed.

- *What will you say to William?*

Edith felt the rich wool sleeves as she wrapped the cloak around her. It had been two days since the Coronation. Heady days where she had accompanied her husband to Westminster Abbey and they had together been crowned King and Queen of England. In the back of her mind she was afraid that it had all gone too well, had been too simple. Over the Channel, the Norman Duke was roaring, she was certain of it. And he would come.

- *What should a king say to a duke – and a bastard Duke at that?*

- *He will not rest easy in Normandy, Harold.*

- *Let him come. Even the Northern men who hate us, will not stomach the Norman Duke coming to rule them. He will be no match for us.*

211

HARALD HARDRADA - THE LAST VIKING

Harold took Edith's hand in his, a small petite hand, pressed it to his lips and kissed it.

- *It is done, Edith. It is over, and there will be no blood. William will not dare to come against us.*

- *And what of your brother Tostig? Will he not challenge your right to be King?*

- *I shall send for him, give him land and dominion over the North. He shall benefit from the Godwinson rule. All will be well.*

And Edith smiled at her husband. They were King and Queen and nothing could destroy them now.

- *Norway was never enough.*

Torah had found Harald alone. The English King's brother had landed and Harald waited for him here in the large hall where he greeted all the important visitors: ambassadors from Sweden and Denmark had stood here, and soon it would be the Saxon Earl, Tostig.

- *Is England worth such a risk, Harald?*

He turned to her. His smile was as broad as his chest and he held his arms open to her.

- *My dear Torah. I love Norway, and my heart will always be here, but my feet itch and my eyes wander beyond these familiar fjords.*

- *And if you have to fight for it? Are you not sick of fighting?*

- *Look at this face, Torah.* He took her fingers, and placed them on the scar that ran diagonally across it.

- *This is a face of a warrior. It is time for me to earn some new scars.*

- *And what if the scars are so deep they will not allow you to return here.*

HARALD HARDRADA - THE LAST VIKING

- Norway is at peace now; we have sons who will rule well over it.
Torah bit her lip. She had a head full of words but she knew she could not say them. This was *her* doing; Elisiv. She and the queen had grown closer, and she knew her mind. It was her restless soul that infected Harald. She remembered how keenly she had felt the rebuff to her brother-in-law's claim. Edward had assumed that he would become the heir to England, that he would now rule England, giving Elisiv – and therefore Harald – the opportunity to wield power over the country.

- What is so special about England, that you would risk your life for it?

- England wields great power, Torah. For a small country it has much to offer us, here in Norway.

Torah saw the lie for what it was.

- You are like a small boy, Harald, who when he is told he cannot have a toy, will do everything he can to take it.

She saw his face darken then and she knew she had hit home.

- It is mine, Torah, through my brother's line. England is mine, and I will not allow others to rob me. I am a soldier, and giving up without a fight is not in my nature.

The storm blew over as quickly as it had come, and the smile returned. He held her close.

- Beside, there is no risk. With Tostig Godwinson fighting alongside us, we will soon smash the Saxons into submission.

Unseen by either of them Elisiv had entered behind them:

- And you, too, sweet Torah, will have what you want. Magnus will be King here in Norway and the Torbergs will rule this country. Isn't that what you always wanted?

Torah turned to face the queen.

- Harald was all I wanted, and to be by his side in Norway. What is England to me?

213

HARALD HARDRADA - THE LAST VIKING

- You will never understand this man, Torah Torbergsdotter. But I understand him, understand his needs. You have borne him two sons and they will carry his name throughout history, here in Norway. But our children will take his name beyond these shores. Our children will stretch beyond Norway, beyond England even. As far as Vinland. That is his dream. Then the skalds will sing his name and recount his deeds till the end of time. It's immortality he seeks, isn't that right, Harald?

The King placed an arm around each of their waists and roared with laughter.

- The gods must truly love me to have given me two such women to guide me.

Tostig arrived later that evening.

The two men sat together in the hall, finishing the last of the banquet that had been prepared. All the others had gone, leaving the two men alone.

- You may know the English, Godwinson, but you do not know Norway's men. We are not here to support your claim. They will follow me to Valhalla if that's where the journey takes them. But they will never follow you. People here say that the English are not to be trusted. Forgive my blunt speech.

- Is it true, that Magnus, your nephew sent messengers to King Edward that England was rightfully his, sworn to him in a treaty with Harthacnut? So why did he not take it? For the same reason that you could not take Denmark.

Harald kept his temper in check, drained his cup, and allowed Tostig to continue.

- You failed to win Denmark because the people were against you. And for the same reason, Magnus knew England could never be his. They wanted Edward.

- All of the people?

HARALD HARDRADA - THE LAST VIKING

- There are some who would follow you, but not enough to be sure of victory; not enough to hold power. But I am a Saxon Earl. They will follow me. With me by your side I can give you the support of many of the chieftains.

- And what of the new king? What of your brother, Harold?

- The only thing I lack is the title King. In all other ways I wield as much power as he.

- And what is your price, Tostig?

- A share of the Kingdom. Give me back those lands that my brother stole from me. Together we are unstoppable. Together we shall conquer and rule England.

Harald spent the night awake, talking with Elisiv, outlining the invasion plans.

- Can this Saxon be trusted, Harald?

- No-one can be trusted when power is on offer, Elisiv, but once we are crowned King and Queen of England, then we can deal with Tostig and his Saxons. England will become a Viking land – all of it. Perhaps we shall rename it Little Norway. And with that done, we shall seek further lands to the West.

They stood locked in an embrace. Their kisses were hard and their bodies felt for each other.

Not all of Norway was as confident as their king. Even in his own court, there were doubters. Unlike Norway, England was very populous. And their reputation for war was renowned. There were still enough who supported Harald – after all his great achievements, nothing would be too difficult. Besides, these Saxons needed teaching a lesson. England was a Viking country held by men who had no right to be there. Recruitment had begun in earnest. Some of the opposition to another war came from those whose levies were increased to pay for it

HARALD HARDRADA - THE LAST VIKING

Tostig left for Flanders in the Spring to muster his troops. War was coming.

HARALD HARDRADA - THE LAST VIKING

OMENS

War was coming. The fleet was gathering at Solund. News had reached across all of Norway. War was expensive for everyone, but it was the poor farmer who paid the highest price. Levies were raised to fund the war, and they had to be paid from the paltry wages earned by the men who worked on rented land as much as by the wealthy owners. And field-hands had to be released to take their places alongside the king, probably never to return.

War was coming. And some saw in it a chance to change their lot. Those who could not afford to pay were told to join the king's fleet. In return they would win their own land, on English soil, enriched with the blood of dead Saxons.

War was coming. And in Ringerike Dag did his best to ignore its call. He had made his promise to Stina. Had he not followed the King far enough? He had spied in England and now he was greying and his joints were stiff. The family farm – not their own, of course, it would never be their own – was emerging from winter and there would be crops to grow, food to take to market, and the five of them, Dag, Stina, Harald, Erik and Karl would need all their efforts to make it pay. He stood, staring out across the white frosty earth and wrapped his arms around his body to keep the cold out. When was it that he began to feel the cold? Caught in his gaze, the three boys – they were men now – were already out in the field, working hard to turn the frozen earth. Would they be taken from them to fight in a foreign land? He didn't hear Stina move alongside him.

- *They are good boys, Dag. They are their father's sons, strong, diligent, honest and brave.*

- *Then they get as much from their mother, Stina.*

HARALD HARDRADA - THE LAST VIKING

He sensed rather than saw her smile. Her hand moved to his shoulder.

- He is your king, Dag, and your friend. You must do what is right by him.

- I have promised to stay. I am too old for war, Stina.

- And what about the boys? He will send for them. Who will keep them safe if not their father? Who will keep the king safe and give him wise counsel? Leave Karl with me. Between us...

- Things will be hard for you. War is hard for those who stay behind as well as those who fight.

- Then you might as well go. The king has promised us land in England. Our own land. We shall have our own farm, and we shall keep what profit we make. For the first time we shall be landowners, in charge of our own destiny...

- But not in our own country... Dag stopped short, aware that his wife was a Dane, living in a foreign land already.

She sensed his unease.

- Norway is my home, now. Denmark was my parents' home. England can be our children's home. Get ready, Dag. Take Erik and Harald and prepare for war. Take care of them, as you took care of your king at Stikelstad. Then come home and take us back to our new land.

Dag went to the mound of earth that was his mother's grave. She had been wise above all people. What would Brenn have said? What guidance would she have given? He sat beneath the tree that shaded the grave and spoke with her. As the sun arced across the sky, its rays glinted on a sliver of metal which reflected into his eyes. He scratched away at the soil. Slowly, the sword emerged. The grip in his hand was perfect, and the blade keen. This was no ordinary weapon. Where had it come from? What was its meaning? He took it in his hands and it moved in his grip so that

HARALD HARDRADA - THE LAST VIKING

it pointed to the west, catching the sun's red rays on its polished blade. Out of the earth, yet still polished! It was a sign. He must go westward. And yet, he wondered: Where had it come from? Had someone placed it there for him to find? And this was a special piece, which fitted his hand like it was made for him. He knew fine work. Did someone want him to go to England? If it was an omen its meaning was clear. But did he really believe that this was a sign? Whatever the explanation there was no doubting the fact of it. It was a fine sword, and it was buried in his mother's grave for him to find. And he had found it. And it was in his hand.

Dag spoke with the boys at suppertime. They were excited – as all boys are – about the idea of war. He showed them the sword he had found and they held it high above their heads.

- It is a sign. I asked your grandmother, and she gave me this sign. We are to leave tomorrow and make our way west to join the king's fleet.

Karl urged his father to take him too.

- You must stay here, boy, to keep the farm going, to help your mother, to be the man in our house.

- And while I am here, tending the farm, my father and my brothers will be war heroes.

- There are no heroes in war, Karl. There are survivors, or there are corpses.

- And what if you are corpses?

- All the more reason for you to be here. How would your mother survive without your strong arms?

They argued long into the night. But the next morning, Karl was already in the fields before his father and brothers left to go west.

HARALD HARDRADA - THE LAST VIKING

Thjodolf Arnasson was no stranger to war. He had served King Magnus, as skald and as soldier. And now he served the new king, Harald. He was the same age, born in the same month, though the years had been less kind to him. His left shoulder sagged from the weight of the rune-sack which he had carried with him wherever he went. He sat now on a clifftop, overlooking the Sound, watching as the sails furled and the fleet seemed to take a life of their own. It grew by the hour, as the king's warriors assembled. News from England had been defiant. Godwinson would never give up his claim, and Harald would have to take it from him by force. But Harald was a warrior-king. Nothing would give him greater pleasure than ripping England from the Saxon's grasp. And he would be there to see it happen; a witness and a recorder. They had returned from Nidaros earlier in the day. There, with the King he had visited the shrine of St Olaf – the king's brother. Together they had taken trimmings of the saint's hair and nails, and pouched them in a leather sack, which Harald now wore around his neck. They would keep him safe, keep them all safe. Then they'd sailed south to join the army gathering here at Solund. He had heard there were more than two hundred ships. An invasion army with its supply ships, ready to join forces with Tostig's fleet, another one hundred strong so rumours had it. As the sun began to set, and the cold began to bite into his bones Gyrdir came to him.

- *I have had a dream, Arnasson. A warning to the King.*

The poet took out his tools and listened to the soldier, who he knew was close to the King.

- *Tell me what you saw, Gyrdir, and I will make sure the king is warned.*

It had taken great courage for Gyrdir to come to him. Thjodolf knew that the king would not want bad dreams to haunt his

HARALD HARDRADA - THE LAST VIKING

passage. Gyrdir sat alongside him and faced out to sea as he spoke.

- *I was on board the ship. We were nearing an island, perhaps it was England itself. A huge giantess, ugly, wart-covered face, stood astride the harbour entrance. In one hand she held a huge knife, in the other a trough. I could see across the whole fleet, and on every prow there sat a bird – ravens or eagles - and the giantess was crowing like a bird, and inviting the king to fill up the English graveyards, so that her carrion birds can feast on the brave Norwegians.*

When the skald had finished writing, he turned to the sailor.

- *Leave this with me, Gyrdir. I shall tell the King. I shall pass on your warning.* But Arnasson knew he would not. When Gyrdir left, the poet pouched the story and left it there. Perhaps this would be his last journey. Perhaps he would end up in a grave in a foreign country. If so, it was his lot. He was the king's skald, and he would follow wherever he was led. And if he died beside his king, so be it.

But the story would not sleep. Another soldier came to him. He had to tell someone, he insisted. But the king was in no mood to hear his story. He too had seen the ogress, but it was during a battle, for England he was certain. She led the defending army, astride a wolf, which carried a human carcass in its bloody jaws. The wolf devoured it, then another appeared and then another, the wolf gulping down the Norwegian warriors.

- *And all the while the ogress was chanting 'I see the doom awaiting Harald.'*

Two such omens were a worry for the skald. Surely he had a duty to share them with the King.

- *These are nightmares,* the king said. *They are conjured to make us afraid. They are not omens they are Saxon witchcraft. Pagan sorcery. But I am not to be frightened with stories of ogres and giants. They are tales for children. And if this is sent to frighten us that only shows how much Godwinson fears us.*

Dag, Harald and Erik had met with the king and were given special places on the king's own ship.

- You will be alongside me in battle. You will be the first to claim a piece of English land for yourselves. In honour of your mother and of our friendship, and of your loyal service.

But Harald was not immune from such dreams. And it was Dag he told of the dream he'd had.

- I was in Nidaros, where I met my brother, the sainted King Olaf. Olaf spoke to me. He warned me about leaving Norway. He foretold my death on foreign shores.

- And what will you do?

- Do?

- Will this deter you, make you stay here, and be content?

- I can never be content, Dag. You, you of all people know my spirit. I am a warrior, born to fight, born for adventure? And if there is any truth in these visions, these dreams, then let my enemies come. England is my destiny. Elisiv and I were born to rule there, and no phantoms that come in the night will break our resolve.

The time was upon them. The ships were ready, and Harald went to the palace. He would not return to Norway for some time. If the omens were to be believed, he would never return. He must set things in order. He went first to Torah. He held her close, kissed her hard on the lips, felt her round body beneath him.

- There are tales everywhere, Harald. This is a misadventure which could cost Norway its king.

- Norway shall have a new king, Torah. I will proclaim Magnus as my heir. He shall rule in my stead. If I die on the battlefield, Norway will be safe in his hands, safe with you to guide him. If I do

not die, then I shall proclaim myself King of England and I shall send for you. I shall take Olaf to fight alongside me, as I fought alongside Olaf at Stikelstad. He will be my successor there. And together we shall triumph. The pagan Saxons will never beat us for God is with us.

- Take good care of our son, Harald. He is precious to us.

And he kissed her again.

He found Elisiv in the Queen's Chamber. They embraced, and their kisses too were hot, and he longed for her body again. But he held her away from him. She looked at him and stroked his scar with her fingers.

- This is our day of destiny, Harald. Take us with you.

- To battle, Elisiv?

- I would fight beside you, but I will stay at Orkney with our girls, until you send for us. From Orkney it is a short step only to join you on the throne. Let the Saxons swallow their own blood and let them see their King and Queen crowned together. In God's name.

- Bring Maria and Ingegerd to me. Let them kiss their father, and then let them join you on one of the ships, behind the main fleet. We shall be together in Orkney, before the invasion begins.

And so it was done. Magnus, with Torah behind him, took the throne in Norway and Olaf joined Harald on the fighting ship, Ormen, the Serpent. And alongside them **Thjodolf Arnarsson, to record his King's great victory.** Olaf was given command of the bravest and best alongside his father. And further back, with the supply ships, Elisiv, and her daughters, sailed out of Solund.

Their first landing was made in Shetland. Most of the ships continued onward to Orkney where they stocked up with water, and there they were joined the loyal Earls and more ships. The Viking warriors slept soundly in makeshift camps, waiting for the king and the final assault. In Shetland, Harald and Elisiv stayed the night, and Harald held a council of war, outlining his plans to his most trusted warriors, the generals who would lead the men in battle. They pored over maps, talked long into the night with Dag who told them what he had seen, and assured them of the welcome they would receive.

- From Orkney, we shall use the safety of the coastline of Scotland to sail to Cleveland, which will be our first landfall on English soil. There we shall show our might. There will be plenty of riches to be had and word will travel down the coast that we are coming in force and we are to be feared. There will be little resistance. There is no army there to face us.

Then they sailed onward to Orkney, stopped long enough to join the fleet, and there Harald and Elisiv parted company.

- I will send for you. Soon. Watch for the ship that will bring you all to me.

And while Elisiv and Ingegerd kissed the King, the younger daughter, Maria, wrapped her arms around his legs, tears running down her face.

- Stay with us, papa. Stay here where it is safe. I am afraid.

Harald lifted her high upon his shoulders and carried her to the top of the crag that overlooked the bay where the ships sat awaiting his return.

- There is nothing to fear, Maria. Watch for me, you will see fires in the night – this will be England burning. And then I shall send for you and you will marry Eistein Orri, that great warrior and friend, and you will be a Princess of England.

He placed her down on her feet, and she wrapped her arms again around his legs. Elisiv took her hand and led her back to join her sister.

- She is her father's daughter. She will wait for you, anxious until we can be together again.

HARALD HARDRADA - THE LAST VIKING

And in a final embrace, Elisiv and Harald stood, their bodies together forming silhouettes above the bay. And in the distance they heard the shouts of the men, cheering and whistling.

They stayed there on the cliff top: Elisiv, Ingegerd and Maria, watching until the ships were on the horizon. And they saw the giant raven moving at the head of the huge fleet as it sailed into the setting sun. To their left, in the northern sky, they saw the familiar green and yellow lights.

- It is a sign, girls. See. These lights are a sign that wherever we go, the Northern Lights will follow us. Norway will be successful.

They stood and bowed their heads in silence, before making their way back to the rough hall that would house them until they were called. On their ships, the sailors watched the lights too. Amongst them Dag, on the k ing's ship. It was a good omen – at last!

Cleveland fell quickly. The ships were laden with plunder and the men gorged their lusts on the Saxon women. Their numbers swelled as farmers, who still bore the names of their Viking ancestors, joined them, armed with scythes and poles. The first resistance they met was at the town of Scarborough. Men stood on the hill above the town inside the wooden fortress. They fired arrows down the hill onto the heads of the invaders, poured boiling oil down over the rocks, but after two days of fierce fighting Harald stood on top of the rock and built a huge funeral pyre, then used it to hurl burning faggots onto the town itself. Houses caught fire and the smell of charred and rotting corpses filled the air, even overpowering the smell of salt air. More booty was seized, more women were raped, and the earth of the streets was stained red with blood. The English knew they had little choice. If they wanted to live they must submit. And the Vikings made their way south before joining their ships again and sailing south to Holderness and the great estuary of the Humber. There he met with Tostig's assembled fleet, which had crossed from Flanders.

Northern England was his for the taking now.

1066

HARALD HARDRADA - THE LAST VIKING

THE FORCE GROWS LARGER. Dust clouds swirl around them and soon we are enveloped in it, choking and coughing. Harald and Tostig are standing together. The looks on their faces show how the attack has come as a surprise. Word has reached us. It is the English King's army, led by Harold himself, up from London, gathering force as they marched northward. Tostig wants to retreat, back to the ships, but the king refuses. Three are sent back, all of whom are known to me; brave and sure riders. They will return with the rest of the men, and our armour. The Landwaster banner is raised and we stand and wait in a long thin line of resistance, with the wings bent backward so as to make a circle, with shields interlocked, above and in front of us. Our wall of armour. Inside the circle stands King Harald, and I stand alongside him with other handpicked soldiers, and Tostig and his company beside us. In this way we shall repel the cavalry charges. Spear shafts are set into the ground, points aligned with the horses' breasts, to form a defensive wall. Archers were also with us. They will release their arrows onto the heads of the defending army. As we stand in these positions, ready to fight to the death if it is required of us, King Harald rides round the lines, inspecting the formation. He sees me and removes his helmet. There is a smile playing on his lips. 'We are ready, Dag. As we have always been ready, you and I.' And I nod to him. Yes. We are ready. As he wheels the horse around, he is thrown to the ground. I make a move towards him, but he holds up his hand: 'It is a good omen. A fall is a fortune on its way.' Does he believe that?

The enemy send a small troupe to speak with the king but they are not there to make peace. They tell Harald he must return or the only English land he will have is seven feet of ground: for he is taller than most men. But I know this king. There will be no retreat. As

HARALD HARDRADA - THE LAST VIKING

he watches them return, Harald asks Tostig who their leader was. When he learns that it was Tostig's brother, King Harold himself, he shakes a fist at their retreating backs. 'If I had known who he was I would have killed him where he stood.'

The battle is coming and Harald addresses the men. We fear the worst; our only hope lies in our army returning in time from the ships. 'We go forward into battle,' he tells us, 'without armour against their blades.' The poet Thjodolf stands before us:

> **Were this mighty King to fall,**
> **If we cannot stem the tide,**
> **He and his heirs are in our hearts,**
> **Our bodies here reside.**
> **The two young eaglets will avenge**
> **The death of the brightest sun.**
> **Never shall we abandon them.**
> **God's will be done**

HARALD HARDRADA - THE LAST VIKING
BATTLE

The battle began. It started as they knew it would, with a cavalry charge. But Harald's Vikings met it without flinching. Harald had organised the field of battle; the stakes lined up with the horses' chests as they tried to break the line, and the archers fired a rain of arrows on their heads. The Saxon cavalry charged and fell back, not once, not twice but many times that first day. Each charge left more bodies on the ground, more blood on the riverbank. But it was the English who lost more men. At the end of the day, the wounded Norwegians were brought back inside the ring and given what help they could, which was little enough. Harald called his generals to him, Dag amongst them.

- *Their assaults are half-hearted. These English warriors are no match for us. Before the sun is up, we shall launch our own attack.* And so it happened. And as the cavalry returned, and again retreated, the Vikings broke ranks, opening their shield-wall, and followed the retreat. The trap had been set, and as soon as the shield-wall was broken the English cavalry rode down through their lines, coming from all sides with spears and arrows showering Harald's army.

Harald saw the trap too late. But he was not a man to retreat. God would bring him victory against the Saxon heathens. With Dag at his side Harald rode into the area of thickest fighting, his sword swinging in two-handed grip, mowing a path before him. His anger drew him on, and Saxon after Saxon fell at his feet. Nothing could bar his way. Even without his armour – still a long way behind his lines – his heart never wavered. Alongside him, the bravest and best fought with every ounce of strength. But even as they struck blows, they knew it was hopeless.

HARALD HARDRADA - THE LAST VIKING

Both armies drew back to reform, and there was a long lull in the fighting. Dead bodies were reclaimed and piled high. Weapons and helmets were recovered, and new owners took them. Then the battle started again. Harald led the charge. The Viking numbers were low, but they fought with such bravery that they killed twice their number before they lay dead. Night had fallen, and the fighting continued. In the early morning, they were still there. Dag knelt, fending off the blows of an axe-wielding English soldier. The king stood alongside him, swinging his sword in giant arcs. Dag thrust his sword deep into the man's belly and, as he climbed to his feet, he heard the arrow fly past him. He would later say that it was all in slow motion.

The sun had not yet risen on Orkney. Elisiv felt it in her bones. The battle had started. Soon Harald would send for them, and they would sail up the Thames to meet him at Westminster where together they would be crowned, King and Queen of England. Just as she had dreamed. She saw Maria standing in the doorway of the barn that served as their home, a waiting room.

- *The lights are brighter, mama. Perhaps it is a sign from God that my father has destroyed the English.*

- *Wait for me here, Maria, while I get dressed. We shall watch the dawn and count it as our first day as rulers of England.*

Maria heard nothing of her mother's words behind her. She opened the doors wider and moved out into the dew-sodden meadow and pushed her way past long bent grasses, closer and closer to the parapet that stood guard over the village. If she could only climb a little higher, to the top of the tower, say, she might be able to see England. Her new home. Perhaps she would see her father, tall and brave, wielding his sword, his yellow hair catching the early sun's rays. Hand and foot in consort she climbed the wall. At each step a piece of masonry would slip to the ground. She stopped for a moment and looked back. Her mother and her older sister were running towards the castle. They were shouting her name. They would climb too. She resumed her ascent, ignoring the falling stones, each step taking her closer to the top. When she looked back again, her mother and sister were tiny below her feet. Up, up, up she went, until at last her fingers scrabbled with the loose stones that lay atop the wall. She clambered up and stood high above the ground.

They looked up at her, waving their arms. And Maria looked back at them, laughing, and pointing in the direction of England to where her father stood victorious.

- Climb up, mama. Climb up. Papa waits for us to wave at him.

Down beneath her, they could only watch as she lost her footing and started her descent, flying through the air towards them.

Thjodolf died on that day too, alongside his king. Neither man saw the arrows that took his life. All that remained were his words, carved into the leather:

> *Disaster has beset us.*
> *Harald is dead.*
> *Our king lies broken,*
> *An arrow in his head.*
> *Our mighty Viking King*
> *Has fallen where he fought.*
> *His claim to England's throne*
> *Is ended. Come to naught.*

HARALD HARDRADA - THE LAST VIKING

Dag found prince Olaf in the field. He was wounded but stood defiant.

- Come, Olaf. The battle is lost. We must take your father's body back home, just as we did your uncle at Stikelstad.

Together they lifted King Harald's body and Dag carried it away from the battlefield, borne on his back, up the hill. His friend, his king was dead. He had chased a dream and now that dream was broken. But his body must be taken home. His son and heir must be saved for Norway. The Viking army fell back when they saw the banner fall. The king's body must not be trampled underfoot, must not be left to feed the crows and dogs.

Beneath them Tostig and Harold met, the Godwinson brothers face to face. Harold offered him his life if he would cease, if he would surrender.

- We shall fall beside our True King, sharing his fate. We shall not beg to your Saxon soldiers for mercy. I would rather die than surrender.

And they had their wish. Bodies fell in great numbers until the resistance was broken and Harold Godwinson raised his standard above the battlefield. The battle here in the north was over, but already there was rumour that William, the Bastard Duke, was sailing from Normandy. There was no time to lose.

Elisiv held Maria's broken body in her arms. The limbs hung loose, like the rag doll the girl kept on her bed. The fall had crushed her. And Elisiv felt it crush her too. Somehow, she knew... The moment of *her* death had been the moment of *his* death. She was not only the mother of a dead child; she was a widow too.

233

HARALD HARDRADA - THE LAST VIKING

Vilomah, she had heard it called. And she was stranded here in Orkney.

The Viking reinforcements arrived too late. Dag and Olaf watched them below their position on the hill above the river. Their armour shone in the warm sunlight. Their leader, Eystein Orri, picked up the Landwaster banner and fighting began again. Harold Godwinson was desperate to end the battle. The English army had a long march south but could not leave until the last of the Vikings was dead. The Saxon army attacked with renewed vigour, avenging the soldiers who had suffered at their hands and finally the Norwegians collapsed, bloodied: exhausted or dead. It was dark before the battle was finally over. The stragglers from the defeated army made their way up the hill. The English army was already gathering.

Night came and morning followed. When Dag and Olaf returned to the ridge's edge and looked down the English army had gone. Even from here the river seemed red, Saxon and Viking blood mingling in the cold waters.

- You must return to Orkney and from there home – with the queen and your half-sisters. Norway has need of a strong prince, serving alongside your brother. There will be many who, now that your father is dead will try to wrest Norway from your brother's hands. Together you can keep our country safe and free.

- I must take my father's body home.

- Leave him with me. I will find him a temporary resting place until it is safe for him to return. Trust me. I shall bring him back to you for proper burial.

HARALD HARDRADA - THE LAST VIKING

- Of all men, my father trusted you most, Dag Gaarder. Now I, his son and heir will trust you too. Keep his body safe. Then return him to us as quickly as you can.

Orkney in Autumn should have been beautiful. But for Elisiv the bright sunshine and warmth mocked her misery. Her daughter had died, and now her husband too was dead. She longed for her own turn to join them. What was she if her Harald was dead? For months now she had felt the cold clutch at her breast and knew that her death was not far away. Now, with these twin tragedies, what was there to live for. First, she must secure a good marriage for Ingegerd, one worthy of a Norwegian-Rus princess. She greeted Olaf warmly, but Olaf was not her son. Nor was he his father. It seemed to Elisiv that she had lost almost everything while Torah... It was unfair of her to think such things, but the grief was painful, more than she could bear, and her gratitude for Olaf's safe return was no compensation for her losses. Maria's body was wrapped for transporting for burial in Norway when they could return. She longed for the day when she could receive her husband's body. Already her mind was racing ahead to how the dead king would be buried alongside his daughter Maria at the Cathedral in Nidaros in the church dedicated to Christ's holy mother. Messages were sent to Oslo, and Olaf, Ingegerd, and Elisiv waited for more boats to return. Olaf shared his plans with his stepmother.

- We shall wait until Winter has passed. Orkney will keep us safe until then. I shall return to Norway in the Spring and, there, rule alongside my brother. I will take the title of King on my return.

Dag sent a message to Orkney too.

HARALD HARDRADA - THE LAST VIKING

The body is safe. King Harold has given his assurance that our dear king's body can be returned to his home. But the weather conspires against us. We may have to stay here, near Scarborough, for the winter and then we shall journey with you back to Norway. Please send messages to what is left of my family, to Stina and Karl. Both my sons, Harald and Erik died brave men's deaths and had a Viking funeral. I shall return to them in the Spring and spend the rest of my days with them, a husband and father.

Elisiv thanked the messenger.

- Dag Gaarder has been a good friend to my husband. A loyal subject throughout his life. Tell him we shall pass on his messages, and we shall await his arrival with his friend's body in the Spring.

There were other plans to be made too.

She found Olaf in the small church that stood close by, and she sat alongside him as he prayed. As he raised himself from his knees, she touched his arm.

- There is something you must do for me, Olaf. Something you must promise me.

- Ask anything of me Mother Elisiv. You have my word I shall do whatever I can. My father loved you and you were Queen of Norway. I owe allegiance to you on both counts.

- My heart is weak, Olaf. And I fear it may not last beyond the next year. There are things still left to resolve. Your father's burial plans – alongside Maria in Nidaros - may be my last act, if I live that long. But I worry about Ingegerd. She has been betrothed to Olaf, Sveyn's son, as part of the peace treaty between Norway and Denmark. See that he keeps his promise. She must be provided for. She is the grand-daughter of Jaroslav the Wise, as well as daughter of King Harald. Nothing less than this marriage would be right for her.

HARALD HARDRADA - THE LAST VIKING

- You have my word on it, Mother Elisiv. I shall oversee the preparations myself, if necessary, but I hope your fears are for nothing and that you live long enough to see all these things come to pass.

Elisiv touched his sleeve, smiled at him, and returned to the body of her daughter. Later, she told Ingegerd what she had asked of her stepbrother, and as she lay in bed that night, she felt at peace.

1067

HARALD HARDRADA - THE LAST VIKING
HOME

Yuletide was almost over. Dag and the small band of Vikings kept their whereabouts secret to all but their closest allies.

- England is a small country and much more accessible than our own Norway. There are long straight roads left behind by the Roman troops. News travels quickly here.

Messengers came to Dag regularly, and from them he learned of the fate of Harold Godwinson's army. Already weary from the battle at York and marching southward to the Channel coast, they had been defeated by the Norman Duke. Harold was dead and the new king, once known as Duke of Normandy was wearing the crown. The first King William of England, crowned on Christmas Day in the great abbey at Westminster. Nothing had been said about King Harold's pledge to allow Harald's body to be returned to Norway, so they stayed in hiding near Scarborough, the body wrapped in preserving sheets, the Raven flag blanketing him, his armour laid by his side. Dag trusted his hosts. They were Vikings, had little love for Saxons, and none at all for the conquering Normans.

- These Normans are our cousins. If not by blood, then by descent. These Norsemen, as once they were called, sailed alongside our great grandparents. Surely he will allow us to bury Harald's body with the dignity and grace he deserves?

But he took no chances, and stayed hidden throughout the snowy months.

On Orkney, the first signs of Spring had arrived. Throughout the Winter, Olaf had kept watch, for signs of ships from the English

HARALD HARDRADA - THE LAST VIKING

coast. None came. He and Elisiv and Ingegerd had set up home, a court in exile. He saw how Elisiv grieved the two deaths that had befallen her since she arrived at these storm-ravaged islands. He watched as her body bent and her soul sagged. He hoped he could get her back to Norway before she died. Ingegerd, a beautiful woman now, of twenty-one, would be married to Olaf, and when he inherited the Danish throne, she would become Queen. It is what Harald and Elisiv had wanted, and he would make sure Sveyn did not renege on his promise. By force if it was needed. When the first frosts had gone; when the icy rivers and lakes began to melt; when the green shoots began to appear, he was ready to return home.

- *It is time, Mother Elisiv. Time to return to Norway. I fear that Sveyn may attack us now he knows that my father is dead. And alone, Magnus will be no match for him.*

But Elisiv was reluctant to go East without her husband's body.

- *We should wait until Dag Gaarder returns. Then we can all travel together, you, your father, your step-sister and me. Surely that will be safer?*

- *I want to return. I want to take up my rightful claim, and to share the Kingdom of Norway with my younger brother. I have been away from home for too long.*

- *But Olaf...* He held up his hand, the palm towards her face. And in that gesture, in the set of his face, the stance of his body, Elisiv saw that he was indeed his father's son and would brook no argument.

- *We shall go. As soon as we can load our ships. The weather is kind to us, and we must make good use of it for a safe and speedy return. And we must ensure that the Danish King will keep his bargain, to link our families together. King Harald will not be long behind us.*

HARALD HARDRADA - THE LAST VIKING

Ingegerd's marriage was too important to Elisiv. She saw the need to return, but she had so hoped to take her husband's body home. It was almost summer when they finally set sail. There had been no sign of Dag Gaarder, but they would wait no longer. They had all been away from home for too long.

At almost the same time that Elisiv arrived in Norway, her husband's body was lifted onto a great Viking ship. At its prow was the carved serpent, and high above its mast flew the Raven. Harald was going home, and it was Dag Gaarder who would bring him there. The ship carrying his body sailed directly to Nidaros and waited there for the royal party to welcome his body at the great cathedral.

Olaf had joined his brother and together they rode out against the Danish army, led by Sveyn who, just as Olaf had suspected, saw a chance, with Harald dead, to expand his power and reach.

Like, Hardrada, his father before him,
Young Olaf stood ready to fight.
No King had the courage to take from him,
This land that was his by right.
In one hand he held a sword,
In the other a flag of peace.
Denmark could choose between them!
- And at last their battles ceased.

He had achieved what his father had never done. Peace with Denmark. Not since the days when King Magnus reigned could Danes and Norwegians sleep safe in their beds.

HARALD HARDRADA - THE LAST VIKING

And later that year, when both kings attended the wedding of Ingegerd, their half-sister, to King Sveyn's son, Olaf, the three men shook hands and signed a treaty.

Torah smiled to herself. All she had ever wanted was to see Norway at peace and she delighted in her sons' victory. Torah was the mother of kings. Harald's line would stretch out into the future of Norway, and she, Torah would have played her part. Harald's body was in Nidaros, buried there by the shrine of the sainted Olaf, his brother. Alongside him was buried Maria, the child whose death on Orkney coincided with his own. Torah had to support Elisiv in the great Cathedral. When the ceremony was over, when the great feast was done, and when they returned home, Torah welcomed Elisiv in her rooms in the palace at Ánslo. Torah sat beside her, and listened as she spoke softly and slowly:

- *Torah. You and I, who should have been enemies, have laid aside our differences. We have learned to live together in this palace, both married to a great Viking King. You will outlive me...*

Torah laid a hand on her arm, feeling the tears well behind her eyes.

- *... I know my death is close at hand. I thought at first to be buried at the side of my husband, but I ask instead to be allowed to return to Kiev, to my parents' home, there to be buried.*

Torah held Elisiv tight in her arms and allowed her tears to flow. This woman, once a bitter rival for Harald's love, had become a friend, a companion, and her Queen.

- *You shall be taken there, Queen Elisiv. I shall see it done.*

Dag Gaarder kicked the side of his horse. He could see the farm ahead of him, could make out the strong body of his youngest son,

HARALD HARDRADA - THE LAST VIKING

Karl, and alongside him his beloved Stina. He felt the trot become a gallop and he yelled her name into the wind.

- *Stina. I am home.*

Conquest 2 – Harold Godwinson – The Last Saxon
Due to be published in paperback and e-book versions in 2023.

A preview of the opening chapter follows.

Conquest 3 – Duke William of Normandy - The Bastard
Due to be published in paperback and e-book versions in 2024.

HARALD HARDRADA - THE LAST VIKING

ACKNOWLEDGEMENTS

As always there is a list of people to thank...

To Linda, who, as she has so often, read the developing story and kept me going with her kind words and supporting comments.

To Friends and Fellow-writers in The Retford Authors Group, who spurred me on with their encouragement, and who enjoyed my success as much as I did.

To the writers of sagas and biographies that were constantly perused so that I could be as accurate as possible.

CONQUEST 2

HAROLD GODWINSON

The Last Saxon King

Barry Upton

On Amazon Bookshelves at the end of 2023.

HARALD HARDRADA - THE LAST VIKING

I know what they say of me. All of them, even my own family. That I am self-seeking. That I am ruthless. That I will stop at nothing to get my desires. But their "ruthless" is my "determined". I have a solemn duty to ensure that this land of ours, this England, remains a Saxon land; that it will never again be subject to the whims and taxes of a foreign king. We have had our share of Viking warlords. I will fight them with the last drop of my blood. We have had enough of their heathen ways.

And now there is talk of a Norman invasion, as if England deserved no better than a bastard Duke. And all because of a promise made by a weak king in a moment of brain-fever. No! It is time that England became what it truly is - a Saxon Kingdom. And who better to bring it about, than a Saxon Earl; and am I not the best, the most noble and the bravest of them all?

Let them say what they wish to say. Let them call me ruthless and self-seeking, but I am Harold, son of Godwin and I am destined to become King of England.

HARALD HARDRADA - THE LAST VIKING

TIDES

- What makes the sea move?

It was a reasonable question from a young boy who grew up in the rolling hills. My brothers laughed at the question. Harold wasn't even the oldest of us! That was Sweyn. But that never stopped him from acting as though it were he and not Sweyn who was the most senior. He was seven years old when I was born and my earliest memories of him are of a sometimes kindly, but more often teasing older brother. I saw little of Sweyn who seemed to spend much of his time in the company of local monks, memorising great chunks of the bible, even learning the skills of illustrated writing. By the time I was old enough to explore the estates, learning to shoot an arrow, to kill a wild boar, to bring down a deer, Harold was already at the court of King Cnut. Three of us, brothers by birth but not by inclination, all led separate lives: the church, the court and the estate. There were times however when all three of us were together.

I was still very young, five or six, I think, but I remember a visit to the wide-open stony beach a few miles south of our home at Senlac.

- It is never still. It is like a strange and restless animal.

Sweyn made no reply. He was alongside the King who had invited his loyal earls and his younger son to join the royal party. Harold who was selecting stones to hurl into the water, watching them bounce on the surface.

- What a dolt you are, Sweyn. The sea is not an animal.

I had him there. Of course, it was an animal. Look how it moved, how it roared.

- It is you who are the dolt, big brother. What can it be if not an animal? See how it moves; listen to the roars; feel its power.

248

HARALD HARDRADA - THE LAST VIKING

But Harold wandered further down the beach looking for thinner and smoother stones. I could hear his laughter coming back up the beach. I felt my mother's hand take mine and pull me back away from the water. And she shouted across to Harold.

- *Tostig is no different from you at his age, Harold. Give him time to grow, to understand.*

But Harold was out of earshot or pretended to be. She brought me back up the beach and replaced my boots which I had removed earlier to keep them from the waves. The king sat on a giant chair out of reach of the water.

- *The king has asked us to join him, all of us. He has a lesson for us.*

King Cnut was a mighty man – or so he seemed to my childhood self. When he was standing, he was head and shoulders above other men, and his strength was well chronicled. His thick woolly beard and the crown perched above his brow made him twice as imposing and I always felt afraid in his company. Father, Harold and Sweyn stood alongside him, among the other earls and their sons. I wanted to tell them to move further back for the sea creature was getting ever closer. I pulled at mother's hand.

- *Can the king not see what is happening? The sea is getting closer and soon it will bite his toes.*

This brought laughter from everyone, none louder than Harold, and I felt the colour rise in my cheeks.

- *Be gentler with the boy.*

It was Cnut who had spoken. I looked up at him and he beckoned me towards him. Father had often spoke of the king; of how he was not an old man, but he would not live much longer. He had travelled far and wide across the seas, even to the coronation of Conrad, the Holy Roman Emperor, to whom we said prayers every day. All this travel, father had said, had weakened him, put a strain on his heart. Soon the kingdoms would pass to Harthacnut, his eldest son who was in Norway attending to the rebels there. Father had said that Harthacnut would make a good king, a strong brave soldier, unlike the king's younger son Harold. *He has a reputation for running away.* I didn't think running away was such a bad thing so long as he was a fast-footed runner.

- I am a king, Tostig, but I recognise the wisdom in your words. This sea, this water creature has so much power.

- But you are a mighty king. You have more power than anyone in this land, more power even than this creature.

- See how wise the boy is. He recognises the power and greatness of his king. I used this creature of his, rode on his back to this very spot where we stand. I led an army of Vikings, two hundred ships and one thousand men, and became King of England. And all on the back of this wild sea creature.

- If you ordered him to retreat, he would be too afraid to bite your toes! You are king not just of England, but of Denmark and Norway too.

- And once of Scotland, but that is another story, eh, boy?

From Harold, I had heard the stories of Scotland. The wild men from the north had raided again and again far to the north, and Prince Harold had led the English soldiers with little success. Eventually the king had given up the claim he had.

- Who can resist you, mighty king? Who can stand against you?

There was more laughter, until Cnut silenced it by raising his hand high. The waves were creeping closer, and I looked at the King's soft leather boots. They would be ruined unless he ordered the sea to halt. Slowly, sedately, majestically King Cnut stood. He was a tall man, but his shoulders were a little bent, and his eyes showed something of the strain it must be to be a king. He turned his back to the water and looked instead at the sea of faces.

HARALD HARDRADA - THE LAST VIKING

- The boy has guessed my purpose. What wisdom comes from your boy, Godwin.

There was no laughter now. And I felt proud. Especially when the king told my father that I was wise.

- I have come to show you how powerful is your king. All of you stand behind me, a little way. All except young Tostig.

He turned back to the water, stretched his hand out to me and I took it. I know he must have felt the shaking, but he held it in his strong grip, and gradually I relaxed. And all the time the sea climbed closer. He saw my eyes looking first at the sea, and then at my new boots.

- What is it, boy? Are you afraid that the king cannot halt this tide? Are you afraid for your boots?

Then he dropped my hand and held both of his arms outstretched, towards the encroaching tide.

- You are subject to me, as the land on which I am sitting is mine, and no one has resisted my right to its lordship with impunity. I command you, therefore, not to rise on to my land, nor to presume to wet the clothing or limbs of your master.

I clapped my hands in delight. Now we shall see the power of King Cnut. This creature will have to turn back. But the sea kept rising and drenched the king's feet as well as my own. Soon it was up to his shins, and I felt the water through the knees of my breeches. He took my hand again and together we walked backwards until we were out of reach. I was dumbstruck. I could say nothing. And in that I was not alone. No-one spoke. This creature had advanced against the king without any retribution, showing no fear of his majesty. Eventually we were on dry stones again, and the king returned to his throne which had been carried back onto drier ground. The king stayed standing, turned to his prince and his earls and called out above the crashing sound of the sea behind him.

- Let all the world know that the power of kings is empty and worthless, and there is no king worthy of the name save Him by whose will heaven, earth and the sea obey eternal laws.

And it was Sweyn who shouted the first *Amen.*

As the son of an earl, whose family was kin to the king himself, I grew up in the midst of intrigue. Harthacnut had not returned. It was Harold who explained it all to me.

- And what is a regent?

- It is someone who rules in the king's place?

- And Harold is the regent?

- Yes.

- Then who is the king?

- Harthacnut. He is the eldest son of the late king, so he will inherit the title.

- But if he is not here...

- That is why Harold sits on the throne. Until Harthacnut returns from Norway.

- And if he doesn't return?

- That is a good question, Tostig. For a young boy!

I had heard my father and brothers talk together. When Cnut died, they had all assumed that the chosen heir, Harthacnut would become king in his place. But he was still in Norway, fighting Cnut's enemies. They thought that Harold "Harefoot" was a poor substitute for his brother but because he was next in line there was nothing else for it. I heard what they said, and remembered it, but at the time it seemed confusing. Father took me on his knee and tried to make it clear, but he was too impatient for my questions, so it was left to brother Harold.

HARALD HARDRADA - THE LAST VIKING

- We are Saxons, descended from a long line of noble families, and now our family sits amongst the highest in England. We are loyal to our king, of course we are, for they give us the power. But we want this country of ours to return again to its Saxon roots, and we are the family to do it, when the time comes.

- But kings are born to rule, is that not so?

- It is, little brother, but it doesn't have to be. It would be better if the wise men of our country, The Witan, took the decision for themselves, so that we are not left with an absent king and a weak regent in his place.

I understood the words, but their meaning was not at all clear then.

There were regular meetings of Wessex earls. They came to our house in Senlac and talked long into the night, long after I was in bed, but the mornings were often full of the discussions that had been held, and I picked up morsels, like crumbs spread on the table. Harefoot had been made king, after two years of waiting for his brother to return. It seems that the same seas that had brought his father to power had brought his stepbrothers to fight against him. My father had stood by the king – however unsuitable he was – and in a fierce battle, the rebels were beaten back into the sea and those that survived fled across it back to Norway. Alfred, one of the king's stepbrothers was captured by my father, and he was brought to Ely where he begged mercy from the king. Blinded and dying of his wounds, Alfred's body was thrown into a ditch, as a clear lesson to others who might try to seize power. Edward, the dead prince's brother had escaped and sailed to join his mother, Queen Emma at Antwerp where he would be sheltered. It was not uncommon for the king to summon my father to court at Westminster. I remember one such time, when Harold and I accompanied him.

HARALD HARDRADA - THE LAST VIKING

- So, Godwin. It is you I must thank that I still sit safe on my throne and English men and women rest easy in their beds.

- We earls of Wessex have always been loyal to our king.

- And in return you have profited much. You have risen to be among the greatest in the land.

- We are loyal, and we receive the king's gifts as reward for our constant, unwavering support.

- Then I have a task for you. I will follow my father sooner than I had hoped. I have had a premonition of my own death, and I want to be sure England remains with my father's blood. There are many abroad who will seek to take the kingdom from us. King Magnus of Norway, or Edward, son of Edmund Ironsides, with the support of Harald Sigurdsson. And others lick their lips across the sea. Find my brother. Tell him England needs him at home. He must take his rightful place as king when I am dead.

Later, in the bedroom I shared with my older brother, I wanted to know more.

- I thought father didn't like this king.

- It is not about liking or not liking, Tostig. You will come to understand this. We must retain our place in the world, keep our power in England. And most importantly, keep the Northern invaders away. Our father is Kingmaker. It is in his hands.

I was beginning to understand how things worked. I was, after all, nearly ten now, and I was learning fast. Harold Harefoot was only king because my father and others like him had supported his claim. *Better a fool in England than a warrior abroad,* is what my father had said.

My brother sailed for Norway. He was going to meet Harthacnut; his mission was to bring the true king back to England.

Printed in Great Britain
by Amazon

25433800R00148